Foundations

Foundations

ABIGAIL STEWART

WHISK(E)Y TIT
VT & NYC

Published in the United States and Canada by Whisk(e)y Tit: www.whiskeytit.com. If you wish to use or reproduce all or part of this book for any means, please let the author and publisher know. You're pretty much required to, legally.

ISBN 978-1-952600-27-2

PART ONE

Her blood ran red like any other warm-blooded American woman, but Bunny knew her insides were inky black, a mixture of oil and water from which she'd never be free. Oil tied her to Texas, to her oil baron family, to her husband, a barrel-chested man as big as the state itself. Water tied her to her mother. And the two co-existed inside her like a quiet disease.

Bunny and her husband had recently left their ranch in the country after finally striking oil on their familial land. The derricks ran all night now, Bunny couldn't sleep and they'd had to trade it for the bright lights of Dallas and a new ranch style home straight out of *Sunset* magazine. Bunny had been given free reign over decorating and each corner of their new home was appointed according to her specific taste.

"Why don't you hire an interior designer?" her sister, Rose, had asked after viewing wallpaper samples together, but Bunny refused.

The walls now displayed a series of labyrinthian illustrations of flowers, varying in each room by color and size of the bloom, until they convinced viewers' eyes that the flowers had picked up an errant breeze, that they were swaying from side to side.

"Someone could get seasick in here," Rose commented.

In response, Bunny just added more layers, a velvet chaise lounge in lavender, different colored glass ashtrays, usually smoldering, were arranged on a low wooden coffee table, a many-paneled sideboard filled with tchotchkes, like a ceramic dog smoking a cigarette while an adjacent ceramic milkmaid bent over to moon any passersby.

The carpet was aquamarine in one room, forest green in another, and a golden yellow brown in the bedroom where the warmer color scheme reminded Bunny of summer. She hung a huge sunburst mirror over their bed, just high enough so that she couldn't see herself in it. The kitchen had a black and white chessboard pattern on the floor, dark wood cabinetry, and a brand new gas range that Bunny bent over to light her cigarettes from as she cooked eggs in the morning. She mixed thick glitter into the ceiling paint and created for herself an endless sky of faux stars.

Her husband traveled for oil industry business, most recently his excursions took him to California. He came home to kiss her on the cheek, switch his suit for a polo, his briefcase for golf clubs, and walk right back out the door.

"It's your own fault for not giving him kids," her sister mumbled over a breakfast of sugared grapefruit and black coffee. Bunny didn't mention that her brother-in-law was also in New York on business, which was why they were eating breakfast together.

It was true though — Bunny was barren and the large house seemed filled with an unnecessary and false hope. Her solution was to get a bird, a parakeet in a cage that sat twittering in the window while she chain smoked on the chaise lounge and read *Vogue* in her floral day wrapper.

She went to the hairdresser her sister recommended on Monday mornings, carefully wrapping her coiffure like a Christmas ham under a silk bandana. She wore the silk bandana all week, unless her husband came home for dinner, on the following Monday she finally took it off and went back to the hairdresser.

Her husband bought her a robin's egg blue Cadillac and

she parked it in their circular driveway to make sure the neighbors saw, to make sure they'd envy her enough to leave her alone. She didn't want any Jell-O fruit salad, no neighbors borrowing a cup of sugar, no having to watch the self-assured neighborhood women pushing strollers, holding their swollen bellies.

She installed mauve drapes in a gaudy Jacquard separating the dining room from the living room. A ruffled valance hung in the entryway; the curtains parted invitingly to a candlelit meal where she tried to entice her husband one evening.

"I made your favorite, pot roast," she smiled at him.

"Oh, Bunny, sorry but I already ate."

"Well, can I at least fix you a drink? A Tom Collins? I have all the right things."

"Gee, I had a few with the boys after work."

"It's only six o'clock."

"We knocked off around two."

Bunny just nodded, wiped her small hands on her pristine apron. Her half-moon nails, painted a garish red, ran imaginary lines down her abdomen like a wound.

"I have a late meeting at the club with Henry, he said he had a client I just had to meet, you know how insistent he can be. So, really, I'm just here to change."

He kissed her cheek on the way to their bedroom, then again on the way out the door, his hands busy knotting a paisley tie.

In the indigo gloaming, Bunny let the candles burn down to nubs and ate an entire pot roast directly from her Le Creuset pan, pausing only intermittently to drink directly from the bottle of Bordeaux she'd bought with her husband's checkbook.

The next day she lay in bed with a cool washcloth on her

head. She'd been sick in the night and the pot roast had made an encore performance. Without turning on the light, she cleaned the bathroom back to sparkling, her husband snoring away on his side of the bed smelling of cigarettes, cheap perfume, and whiskey.

"I feel a little under the weather," she croaked as he got ready for his day.

"Poor Bunny," her husband kissed her forehead. "Take it easy today. Let the housekeeper earn her wages."

He didn't remember the housekeeper came on Wednesdays, it was Thursday. She smiled weakly at him, the Bordeaux still pounding in her ears.

When she heard his car pull out of the driveway, she ventured downstairs in her nightdress and made herself a Bloody Mary with an Aspirin chaser to cut through her hangover. The well-stocked bar should be appreciated by someone, after all. All morning, she played record after record on the new stereo her husband had bought her, until the sun sank low and she went back to bed, alone.

"Why don't you ever drive the Caddy?" he asked some days later.

"I drive it to the grocery store."

"Only twice a week," he huffed.

In addition to the grocery store, Bunny began driving her Cadillac to the library once a week. She read *Catcher in the Rye* at the back of the building where she had a view of the pecan tree grove outside. She snuck a peak at *Lady Chatterley's Lover* and *Howl*, they both left her indifferent. Sometimes a group of young boys would barrel through the bucolic scene, collecting pecans and cracking them open with a youthful violence. It was the same day with a slightly different view.

She wandered through the stacks, picking up books at

random. The librarian never offered to help her and Bunny didn't mind.

Her solitary meanderings often took her to the nonfiction section where she read about the development of the windmill, Impressionist painters, and how to make any manner of aspics. One day she picked up a book on palmistry, *The Hidden Art of Interpreting the Hand.* Bunny read about the head, heart, and life lines.

The life line starts at the base of your palm and arcs upward. Contrary to its name, your life line does not determine how long you will live, but instead tells about your passions, your general well-being, and indicates any major changes you might face.

Bunny looked down at her hand. Her life line did indeed curl deeply across her palm, confidently arcing toward the intersection of her thumb and forefinger. The line itself was cut in half at its center like a river and its tributary. This probably doesn't bode well, Bunny thought.

If you have a long and unbroken life line it means you are a steady, strong, and dependable person. A broken life line means you will certainly experience some sort of upheaval in your life. If the line is a clean break, this change is unplanned. If the line runs parallel with another, it is a planned change.

Bunny looked at her hand again but couldn't decide if her impending upheaval would be planned or unplanned no matter how long she studied the book's illustration.

She left the library that day with the palmistry book tucked under her arm.

Bunny's sister came over the next morning for their shared grapefruit, cut in half and sugared. They ate together at the kitchen table rather than the formal dining room. It always felt a little safer to talk there.

"Let me see your hand," Bunny commanded.

Her sister gave her a funny look, "Why?"

"I want to read your palm."

"Bunny, please."

"I've been reading about it, let me see."

Rose tentatively offered her pale pink palm to her sister. Framed by the two grapefruit halves and offset by Bunny's ostentatious floral tablecloth, Rose's hand looked small and childlike. Bunny took her sister's hand gingerly, like when they were girls.

"You have a long, unbroken lifeline."

"Does that mean I will live a long time?"

"Not necessarily, it means you're a steady person, dependable."

Rose crinkled her nose.

"You still might outlive me though," Bunny joked.

Rose pulled her hand back. "This is silly."

Bunny shrugged and they didn't mention it again. Together they reverted back to staring into the empty space and alternating between coffee, grapefruit, and their cigarettes.

That night, her husband made a rare appearance at home, expecting dinner. Bunny hadn't gone shopping, so she cooked a large sirloin steak that she'd stashed in the freezer and two baked potatoes with sour cream.

"Don't you want a steak?"

"Oh, no. I'm not hungry."

Her husband nodded in an approving manner, he liked that his wife kept trim. Bunny watched her husband eat bite after bite of the medium rare meat until he placed his hands on his stomach and leaned back, his baser urges satisfied.

She poured them both another glass of wine. He smiled

at her almost beatifically, like she embodied every angel in the heavens.

"May I see your palm?"

He held out his large hand unquestionably, taking a gulp of wine as he did so.

His palm held none of the delicate whorls Rose's possessed. It was thick and meaty, deeply lined like the dog-eared corner of a book. Her eyes went directly to his sun line, a broad crease that indicated burnout, a failure perhaps in his career. She looked away. Upon seeing his lifeline, which was so broken it resembled Morse code, Bunny panicked and instead brought his hand to her cheek, then her breast. Her heart thudded against the cage of her chest not from desire, but from knowing too much.

He mistook her trembling limbs for a demure ardor and led her to the bedroom where Bunny fell into the bed like a stone and he sweated over her, smelling of meat. He almost overslept the next morning and chided her gently on his way out the door.

Bunny resolved to return her palmistry book to the library that morning.

Resigned to a day of driving the Cadillac and interacting with people, Bunny fixed her hair and applied her lipstick, she chose a butter yellow day dress and headed out.

The library's foyer, lit by skylights and populated with several fake plants, directed patrons first to the circulation desk, then to the great beyond of the library's hidden bounty.

At the circulation desk, a dark haired woman about Bunny's own age with onyx eyes and bright coral lipstick took off her cat eyed reading glasses and looked up.

"Hello again."

Bunny stared back at her blankly.

"I've seen you in here before. I'm usually shelving when you come in. I'm Maria, one of the assistant librarians."

"I'm Bunny."

"How can I help you, Bunny?"

"I just wanted to return a book."

Maria took *The Hidden Art of Interpreting the Hand* and surveyed the cover. Bunny shrank back a little, she never liked others to see what she checked out, which is why she spent her reading time in the library's many lounge areas. She could safely return the book to its shelf without fear of anyone knowing anything. Besides, she'd heard McCarthy had searched people's library records and she had no desire to be a part of any of that.

"This one is pretty good, but there are a few others you might be more interested in."

"Oh, I think I'm done with all that."

"Are you sure? There are some great books on star charts, tarot, even communing with the beyond."

"Like dead people?"

"Well, spirits."

A Bible verse from Sunday school lessons past came suddenly to her: *And beware lest you lift up your eyes to the heavens, and when you see the sun, moon, and stars, even all the host of the heavens, you be drawn away and worship them and serve them.*

"No, I don't think so."

Maria shrugged and placed the book in the return crate. She resumed whatever task had absorbed her before Bunny's appearance and Bunny, thus dismissed, wandered back toward the shelves by the window and the half-finished Agatha Christie novel she'd left a hopeful bookmark in.

Bunny's day passed in silent contemplation of the other

library patrons as they filtered through the dust motes like moths. A mother and child came in together holding hands, the mother took down book after book, showing it to the child, then replacing them until the game wore itself out and the child began to cry. Every time Bunny saw one of these domestic scenes, she expected something to take hold of her, but it always left her feeling cold. Another man, harried and perhaps on his lunch break, rushed through the lounge area. He had the look of someone pursued and Bunny wondered what on earth he needed so badly at the library. Then, she saw him take a seat across from a young college girl studying, watched them passionately caress one another's hands, then she understood the urgency.

She stood to stretch her legs and browsed the section where she'd found her palmistry book. The books lined up before her included titles like: *The Mysticism of Woman, Analyzing the Stars and Plotting Your Future, Seance: Asking The Final Questions.*

Bunny touched her finger to the last one, then pulled it back sharply.

On her way out, Maria was shelving near the front.

"I was hoping to catch you."

"Me?" Bunny asked.

"Yes, I have this friend and he hosts lectures I think you might be interested in."

Bunny wondered what about her gave off the impression she enjoyed lectures.

"Here," Maria thrust an invitation toward her.

The invitation itself was uniquely styled, black cardstock with turquoise and silver embossed lettering in a flowing script. Bunny was immediately in thrall to the tangible fact of the design, only briefly skimming the information: *Dr.*

Herbert PhD. *requests your attendance at his lecture on spirits and the modern world,* followed by a date and time.

"Where is it?"

"Here, at the library, in our gathering room."

"Okay," Bunny heard herself saying. "I'll be there."

Maria beamed back at her, her dark eyes sparkling. "See you then."

At home, Bunny set the enigmatic invitation on her vanity, propped up by a tub of cold cream. She contemplated it as she removed her makeup that night and reapplied it again the next morning. Who was Dr. Herbert and where had he developed such impeccable taste, she wondered.

Her own party invitations were often the talk of the country club, so many people asked how she'd gotten her rafia bows 'just so,' and yet something about this card felt both elegant and dangerous. Bunny aspired to neither adjective, but found herself irreversibly intrigued.

When the day of the lecture arrived, Bunny spent much of the afternoon contemplating her emerald party dress. It seemed just the right color for such an event and, paired with dark jade bangles and her pearl earrings, she felt confident. I should add a red lip, she decided, just as the phone rang.

"Bunny," Rose's voice whined over the line, "I may need to come over this evening, these children are going to be the death of me."

Bunny pretended not to notice that the tell-tale lilt in her sister's voice meant she'd already opened a bottle of Sauternes.

"I'm afraid tonight's no good, Rose. I am just heading out."

"Where to?"

"A lecture on mythology or something. Do you think my

purple turban hat would be too much with my emerald dress? You know, the one I wore to your Labor Day soiree."

"Yes, it's too much."

Bunny reluctantly placed the hat back in its box and painted on her lipstick, she blotted with a piece of tissue while listening to Rose complain about her children. Bunny could never understand why women who so claimed to so desperately have wanted children were the ones who complained about them the most.

"So sorry, love, but I've got to go. Come over tomorrow if you're feeling up to it."

Bunny placed the phone gently in the cradle, turned on her well-shod heel, and headed out toward the unknown.

The library was eerily lit, like a Jack-o-lantern, when Bunny wheeled the Cadillac into the parking lot. The windows, normally so softly lit with an almost domestic aura, now thrust their garish fluorescent lighting in dramatic columns across the gravel drive. It looked crude, Bunny thought.

She parked the Caddy in the only sliver of remaining gloom and went inside.

The silence of the tomb greeted Bunny in the library's foyer, none of the anticipated sounds of childish laughter or the librarian's soft humming as she checked books in. Goosebumps rose on her arms. The purposefully lit tube lights directed her toward a hallway and a persistent murmur like the buzzing of tiny bees spurred her forward. Voices, Bunny determined, punctuated by someone's sharp laugh. Her small heels clicked on the floor like the swift punctuation of a metronome.

The conference room floor was covered with fuzzy brown carpeting, the walls paneled in a similar brown wood. That lighting isn't doing this room any favors, Bunny thought, a saturated cerulean would really make it feel more alive, maybe with honey colored accents. Her mind began to wander.

"Bunny, you made it!"

Bunny found herself grasped tightly in Maria's arms and, when she was released from the unexpected embrace, she was able to take note of all the other people smiling rather madly at her.

"This is Dr. Herbert," Maria began introductions. "Our illustrious speaker."

The man indicated was in fact at least a full head shorter than her husband and, though perhaps the same age, he was bespectacled and embellished with such a dramatic salt and pepper beard. He looked dainty and Bunny would have mistaken him for much older at first glance. He certainly isn't an oil man, she told herself.

"Hello doctor," Bunny offered her hand, and he shook it limply, his own hand as soft as a kid glove. Yes, she decided, her husband would loathe this man. The realization gave her a small, private thrill.

"We were just about to start, why don't you sit by me in the front," Maria offered.

The small group numbered only about ten, so Bunny couldn't insist there was no need to crowd in front and dutifully took her place beside Maria.

Dr. Herbert stood behind a dark wood podium of the sort Bunny imagined politicians often used, it had a very 'about to address the nation' feel about it. She half expected the *Star-Spangled Banner* to play out of the library's old wartime speakers. No such thing happened of course, only Dr. Herbert began to speak, and Bunny was impressed by the carrying quality of his booming voice. Chatter stopped immediately and all eyes were on this strange little wizard of a man.

"What are spirits?" He began. "Spirits are often intertwined with religion, the concept that the spirit lives on after our body's death and is subject to an eternity of reward or punishment based on our body's time spent on earth, the decisions we made."

Bunny almost nodded, but forgot she was certainly not in church.

"What happens to a spirit that is unsatisfied? A spirit that might still have questions? Because, oh so many of them do. We don't die utterly fulfilled and understanding of our fate. Sometimes we die in a state of incomprehension and leave the mortal plane feeling dissatisfied with our own ending."

Someone discreetly coughed.

"What then happens to those souls, those spirits?"

"They go to purgatory," someone confidently stated.

"Perhaps they do go to an eternal doctor's waiting room to spend an indeterminate amount of time counting out all of their experiences both good and bad, wondering if they could have done something differently. And they're sitting there, waiting and waiting, bored out of their minds."

Bunny recalled her doctor asking her to wait after the secretary forgot to book her in for a check up. She'd had a terrible headache and waited for an unacceptable amount of time before finally being admitted to speak to her doctor. She was so thankful when they finally called her name, she almost burst into tears. If that's what purgatory was in fact like, Bunny wanted no part of it.

"So, the spirits are waiting, they're bored, and they want someone to talk to. What if we could call them back?" Dr. Herbert prompted.

Another cough.

"I am going to discuss in this lecture how, through scientific means, we can understand the particulars of recalling a spirit from the intangible world back to the mortal plane. My personal studies are robustly supported by academic citations I am happy to share..."

Bunny tried to focus on the aforementioned particulars of Dr. Herbert's lecture, the insistence on a particular lighting and mood to welcome a spirit back into the tangible world, the necessity of a medium, someone who is well-versed in the calling forth of the dead, and the physical signs of a successful medium, such as ectoplasm that apparently exudes from a medium when in the thrall of a spiritual trance. Bunny thought that last part sounded rather vulgar.

However, try as she might to focus on the science, her mind wandered wildly into the imaginary world of potential spirits, who would she want to speak to again?

Her mother's image appeared first, of course, the youthful face in her wedding portrait, flashed through Bunny's mind. She suppressed it, they didn't talk about her mother. She and Rose pretended they had no memories, though she was certain they just remembered it differently, so it was easier to pretend there were no memories at all. Not her body wrapped in her white nightdress splayed out around her pale limbs, watery floating memories, and someone pulling her from the lake their grandfather fished in behind the ranch's main house. The lake where Bunny watched Rose catch tadpoles and run barefoot along the wooden dock. Those summer memories were forever altered by their father's warning not to get too close to the water, ever again.

Bunny's eyes had glazed over briefly and Maria nudged her, smiling. Dr. Herbert thanked the participants, one of whom, Bunny noticed, was passed out, his mouth agape. His companion nudged him and he sputtered forward and into an abrupt applause that Bunny joined in.

"What did you think?" Maria whispered.

"Fascinating," Bunny said, realizing she meant it entirely.

A few older women with their long, grey hair in Victorian buns, surged forward to speak with Dr. Herbert and Bunny was left to socialize with the others.

"Wasn't he brilliant? Thank you for hosting," a man addressed Maria.

"He was in his best form tonight," Maria agreed.

Bunny still felt as though she were committing an act of espionage, a betrayal of her strict Catholic heritage.

But Bunny also remembered her mother lighting a votive candle in a red glass holder and setting it on their kitchen stove. When Rose reached for it, their mother slapped her hand. "Don't touch that, it's my prayer candle." She remembered her mother asking Saint Anthony to find her favorite slippers, the butter dish, Rose's teddy bear. Her mother telling them to hold their breath as they passed a graveyard, to throw salt over their shoulder, to say a Hail Mary when they crossed the train tracks.

When the man had faded back into another group, Bunny felt it was safe to ask, "Does Dr. Herbert perform seances?"

"He's more focused on the academic legitimization of the medium's profession," Maria explained.

"So, he's an active participant but not the main attraction."

Maria laughed, a sharp bright sound, "You could say that."

"Have you ever been to a seance?"

"I have."

"And?"

"It's inexplicable, you'd have to experience one for yourself."

"Is this like taking LSD where you have to know somebody to know somebody to ask you? And there's a guide and all that?"

Maria laughed again, "Hardly. Besides, you already know me."

Bunny regarded her new friend, "You're not a medium though."

"Not yet. I still have a lot to learn."

"So, where do you go? Where does it happen?" Bunny lowered her voice to a whisper, though it was probably unnecessary.

"Just people's homes, places we feel welcome and safe. We enter the threshold with open minds and questions for the spirit realm. You really can't control who shows up, so it's good to be prepared for anything."

"Who shows up?"

"Spirit-wise. It's almost downright impossible to summon someone particular."

Bunny knew Rose hosted Tupperware parties in her home, well, she called them 'jubilees.' They were ostentatiously themed affairs where housewives mixed gin gimlets a little too early in the afternoon while the consultant displayed a new array of Tupperware available for them to store a variety of meatloaf, spaghetti, and their cottage cheese with canned pineapple they had for lunch while they snuck another gin gimlet.

Well, this isn't any different, Bunny assured herself. I'd just be the host, Maria the consultant, and I'd get the chance to take out my nice dinnerware. I can try that new turkey and cream cheese pinwheel recipe and serve the white wine no one likes but me.

"What are you thinking, Bunny?"

Maybe Maria would like the wine.

"Well, I was thinking, that I'd like to host one of these soirees. I think my house is a place where people can be comfortable, open, and I wouldn't at all mind meeting one of your spirits."

Maria's dark eyebrows raised in surprise. "You want to use your home as a portal space for spirits?"

"Yes, I'd like to invite these unfortunate spirits into my home, as it were. Well, I suppose they can't be any more unfortunate than the people who are usually there."

Maria called Dr. Herbert over and they conversed momentarily while Bunny clasped her hands together, politely waiting.

"Well, Bunny, I think that would do nicely," Dr. Herbert confirmed.

"Lovely. Only, I wish you'd make the invitations."

The corners of his mustache turned up in amusement, "I'm sure I'd be happy to."

After a quick mental calculation, Bunny called forth a date in the coming weeks when she was certain her husband would be traveling to California. She exchanged information with both Maria and Dr. Herbert, who, in turn, kept exchanging covert smiles with one another that made Bunny wonder if they were lovers.

"That's settled then," she said, collecting her handbag. "I'll see you next week," she added to Maria, who embraced her once more. This time, Bunny allowed herself to return the hug. How long, after all, had it been since anyone hugged her.

That night, she carefully removed her makeup, the lipstick leaving tracks on her chin. The house felt as still as a churchyard and Bunny considered that the spirits might appreciate the effort she'd put in. Perhaps they'd even feel welcome. She also thought about calling Rose, inviting her even, but somehow knew instinctively her sister wouldn't understand.

"Is this about mother?" Rose had asked her when Bunny started going to Mass three times a week, a habit she'd kicked after people kept inviting her to work at fairs and yard sales.

Yes, Bunny thought, it's better not to include Rose.

She pulled on her diaphanous lilac nightdress, wrapped up her hair, and lay down in her empty bed, crossing her hands over her chest like a saint.

The country club was her husband's pride and joy. As evidenced by the fact that he spends most of his time there, Bunny noted to herself. The fact that they'd been able to get in at one club rather than the other didn't interest her in the slightest, every club was the same in her estimate. Whitewashed dining rooms, tables and chairs covered in thick white fabric, always inevitably stained by the time the evening came to an end. They all hosted the same parties, and everyone had the same conversations they'd been having since she first went to the family picnics with her father.

Their club had the superior golf course, her husband confided, all the men at work were jealous. He assuaged that jealousy by inviting them and showing off whenever the opportunity arose.

There were no hills in this part of Texas, so the club's main building sat at sea level, flatly overlooking her husband's first love, the golf course. Bunny had to admit the large floor-to-ceiling windows that stared out over the greens were impressive. She watched some of the greens workers walk along the teeing ground, patching divets and running the sprinklers. Did the club ask them to do so now, to show off, to make sure that we in the clubhouse know we are getting our dollar's worth? She wondered idly what might happen if a golf ball came sailing their way.

That afternoon, a club party was underway. The typical affair, no theme this time, Bunny noted. They'd previously attended a luau that featured a baked ham stuck with rings of canned pineapple, an 'around the world' dinner that had greatly upset her husband's digestion, and the annual Christmas party where Bunny always ended up getting her behind pinched by some drunk salesman or other.

Women milled about in small groups wearing smart skirt suits or day dresses. Bunny wore a white dress of satin covered in delicate pink roses, tight at the waist and flared down to her knees, the square neckline showed off her collarbone without giving anything away. Her nails were shell pink and shiny with lipstick to match. Her husband whirled her about the room on his arm and she made polite conversation with the other wives while she sipped mimosa after mimosa until everything felt pleasantly fuzzy and the conversation flowed around her as though she were but a pebble in a stream.

"Haven't seen you in ages... why, is that little Tom... all grown up is he... yes, yes, I hear they can be difficult at that age, college and all that... my sister has two, after all... aren't these cucumber sandwiches divine... yes, Mary did it again... she's always two steps ahead on the trends... missed you at the last party... well, they're divorcing, didn't you hear... yes, tragic... excuse me, I think I need just one more drink."

The sun shone gaily into their soiree and Bunny couldn't help thinking how it would eventually bleach the carpets. At the makeshift bar, a waiter poured her another drink.

"Just a splash of orange juice this time, I think," Bunny told him.

Champagne was her favorite thing to drink. It felt punishingly celebratory, as though she simply must enjoy herself because who wouldn't be happy with a glass of champagne in their hand.

"Bunny! I was hoping to see you!"

Bunny's senses were assailed by the smell of powder and, frankly, a little too much eu de toilette. The woman coming toward her, she saw now, was Mrs. Emma Johnson, an old family friend. She'd known her mother. Bunny took a bracing sip of her drink.

"Why, Emma, I didn't know you bothered to come to these things."

"Well, you know how Charles likes to show me off."

Her certainly white hair was colored a dark auburn and her eyebrows were tinted to match. She wore an expensive skirt suit of mauve that looked very smart but did nothing for her rather sallow complexion. Her face had held up marvelously through the years though. Egg white masks, Mrs. Emma Johnson had confided to her years again, though Bunny never tried them herself.

"Do you have a lighter? I seem to have misplaced my clutch."

Mrs. Emma Johnson lit Bunny's cigarette and her own.

"How are you, my dear?"

The woman's damp brown eyes beseeched her to say something joyful, to tell her she was wildly happy, or perhaps pregnant, to say anything that Mrs. Emma Johnson could report back to everyone in her father's circle as proof that Mrs. Barbara Ann Taylor was okay and not at all as melancholic as they used to whisper. Bunny recalled those same bovine eyes imploring her father to send her to boarding school because 'a girl needs a woman's influence' and that was that. She didn't get to come home anymore, except for holidays.

"Well, I'm just dandy. How are you? Now, have you entered your delightful pies in the fair again this year? It's certainly your year to win, I can't believe Mrs. Stanford beat you last year with that skinny old cherry thing."

Bunny sipped her drink and smoked her cigarette and let Mrs. Emma Johnson pontificate on the exacting proportions necessary to achieve an award-winning pie, which hers had been twice, unlike Mrs. Stanford, that usurper. Besides Mrs. Stanford used canned cherries, she was almost certain, and canned cherries just had no right winning over fresh fruit, no matter if she made the pastry herself.

The fuzzy feeling overtook Bunny again and she let herself bob slightly above the general din. Her husband, she noticed now, was in conversation with some colleague or other near the bar and almost certainly on his second or third whiskey. Lost in the contrived gaiety of the afternoon, Bunny almost raised her hand and waved to him, until she noticed his eyes were focused squarely on the waitress's bosom. Perhaps I've just discovered the real reason he considers this the superior club, she thought, before turning her attention back to Mrs. Emma Johnson's pies.

In her mind's eye she saw a series of lipstick-stained neckties and collars scented with a perfume that wasn't her own. She watched them quietly, said nothing, the least he could do is avoid allowing his eyes to wander in front of their friends.

Friends, what are friends, Bunny thought to herself. Rose was the closest thing she had to a friend and that thought made her somewhat depressed. She smoked her cigarette and realized the feeling she felt in that moment was loneliness.

"Well, dear, it was so good to speak with you," Mrs. Emma Johnson was saying.

"So good to see you as well."

"I'd better get back over to Charles, he'll be wanting to know where I've gotten off to."

Bunny smiled, nodded. "Of course."

Her mimosa was sadly empty and the fuzzy feeling now threatened to become a headache. She wilted into one of the fabric covered chairs, her dress spread out like a springtime trumpet blossom, fleetingly blooming.

Her husband was suddenly at her side, she hadn't even noticed his approach. Of course, her sitting alone wouldn't do for the perception of his peers. She needed to be glowing, happy to mingle and speak with everyone.

"Here you are, I was wondering where you'd gotten off to."

Bunny almost laughed at how they all mirrored one another and didn't even realize it.

"I'm right here."

"Well, let's make the rounds and make sure we've seen everyone."

Bunny dutifully stood, pressed out her cigarette and took his arm.

"Only, do you mind if I get another drink? Mine appears to have gone dry."

She did end up with a headache and pressed her face against the coolness of the passenger side window as her husband guided the Cadillac back to their circular driveway.

In her current state the house reminded her of the two-dimensional paper dolls she and Rose used to play with, a cutout facsimile of reality. The windows overlooking her perfectly manicured yard were dimly lit from the light they always left on, 'for safety,' her husband said.

She thought also of one of the Edward Hopper paintings she'd seen in the library, *Cape Cod Morning*. A woman in a pink dress straining her entire body toward the window, peering out, as though she might launch herself straight through it. Waiting for something to happen, someone to show up, but there are only trees upon trees upon trees. No one is coming for her.

These two thoughts swam through her head as they walked in the foyer and her husband loosened his tie.

"Well, that was successful, overall. Wouldn't you say?"

"Yes," Bunny mumbled.

"What's wrong with you? You've been in a mood all afternoon. It really doesn't make me look good to have a melancholy wife pouting at the table by herself."

"I was hardly pouting. I was speaking to Mrs. Emma Johnson and then I sat down for a moment, that's all."

"People just notice women alone."

"*People* sure do," she shot back. Her headache weakened her and allowed the venom to seep into her voice.

"And what does that mean?"

Bunny shrugged and walked toward the kitchen. She poured herself a glass of water from the tap and swallowed two Aspirin. She found a banana and began to eat that as well, bananas after drinking were her father's magical hangover cure. That, and a Bloody Mary the next day.

Her husband stood in the archway of their tidy kitchen, watching Bunny eat her banana over the sink. His face crinkled at the sight of her, barefoot and still in her party dress.

"How are you still eating? Didn't you get enough at the club?"

"I didn't eat any of that. Their cook is godawful."

"No wonder you have a headache, you were being snobbish about the food."

"Yes, it's no wonder."

The way he looked at her then, she wondered if she'd cracked the facade just a little too deeply, would he keep arguing? Would they finally argue? A small thrill ran through her. Yes, yes, let's have a real fight! She met his eyes and continued to eat the banana, but he just shook his head and walked down the hall toward her bedroom.

Too bad, she thought.

Bunny finished the banana staring out their kitchen window. There were no trees here, not really, just identical rectangles of grass like a patchwork of earth, sewn together by men who wished only to possess the piece of land they felt they rightly deserved.

She dropped the peel in the trashcan and walked outside to stand on their wooden porch. It was covered and had antebellum style columns. Her bare feet felt their way against the wooden planks and it reminded her again of the dock at their family lake.

No, don't think about that now, you've had too much to drink, she warned herself.

In the dim twilight, mosquitoes buzzed and grasshoppers played their songs. She didn't find as many fireflies here as there were in her childhood. She and Rose used to catch them in jelly jars and place them along their window sill like captured stars. She always wanted to sleep looking up at the stars.

I will tonight, Bunny considered. If he thinks I

embarrassed him sitting alone, I wonder how he'd feel about my sleeping on the roof. She smiled to herself.

The neighbor's light came on, illuminating a woman's face as she stepped out onto an adjacent porch. With a blank expression, the woman lit a cigarette and stared off in the opposite direction. Bunny could see her laundry hanging on the line, the outlines of her house dress.

How have I never spoken to this woman? Bunny suddenly felt badly for her self-prescribed isolation.

A child's voice called out, "Mama!"

The woman turned back toward the house. Bunny thought for a moment the woman might notice her, that they might share a moment of silent kinship, she prepared herself to raise a hand in greeting. But the woman put out her cigarette, squashing it quickly underfoot, then turned back toward the house.

"Yes darling? Mama's coming."

And Bunny watched their porch light go out.

The next morning, hangover free thanks to her banana, Bunny sat at the table gloomily reading the newspaper sections her husband had cast aside before leaving for work.

"Don't expect me home this evening," he told her. He didn't kiss her cheek before he left.

An empty day stretched out before her. Dust motes floated in the late morning sunbeams and Bunny thought idly about cleaning, only to remember her housekeeper would come the following morning. No need to rush about after all, she assured herself.

The phone rang, a vibrating noise that jangled up Bunny's spine. She considered not answering, letting it ring and ring itself into silence, but picked it up for lack of anything else to do.

"Hello?... Good morning Rose... I was just about to make an omelette... Yes, of course you can come over... I only have green onions... See you soon."

Rose's presence, though somewhat looming, would help fill the afternoon, Bunny decided. She turned on the coffee maker, then got out her whisk and began to mix together eggs, cream, salt and pepper.

Across the yard, she noticed movement. She watched from their kitchen window as the woman from last night removed her sheets and towels from the line outside. She folded them neatly and placed them in a stack. Bunny imagined her humming contentedly, wondered if she could find similar satisfaction in fresh cotton. The woman carried the laundry inside and Bunny could see her moving back and forth in the window, one moment putting things away, in the next pass she had a child on her hip.

Rose's heavy knock sounded on the door and Bunny lost control of the bowl of eggs on the counter, splashing it across the avocado colored formica.

"Damn," she muttered.

Her sister's tall angular figure dominated the threshold and Bunny stood back to let her enter.

"What were you doing?"

"Whisking eggs."

"It took you a minute to answer the door."

"I made a little mess."

"At least you can afford someone else to clean it."

"The housekeeper comes tomorrow, unfortunately."

"Well, not all of us have the luxury."

You shouldn't have had three kids then, Bunny thought, but said nothing.

"Come on in, I was just about to put the eggs on. Would you like some coffee?"

Bunny was nothing if not an attentive hostess and Rose, now satiated with a cup of milky coffee, leaned her small hips against the counter and watched her sister expertly flip two omelettes.

"You'd think you'd attended culinary school the way you handle those pans."

"I just watched Mama and Aunt Belinda do it. Do you remember how they'd make omelettes on Sunday? Just like us now."

Rose set her mouth in a firm line, sucking her thin lips back under her teeth. She did not appreciate the comparison. Besides, she considered the sisters to have an unspoken agreement in that they didn't talk about the past, the ranch, the lake. Rose erased that part of her life when she went to boarding school, inventing a new persona for herself. Now, the occasional memories of their idyllic life came back to her and she would sit for a moment considering if they were in fact her own reminiscences or something she'd imagined.

Bunny served up the omelettes on clear glass plates, sprinkling them liberally with green onions and Parmesan cheese.

"This is divine," Rose complimented.

Bunny smiled and moved the green onions around her plate, creating a haphazard spiral pattern, before taking a bite.

"Have you been reading any other palms lately?"

"Not exactly."

Rose raised her eyebrows.

"I've been reading about seances, about calling spirits back from beyond," Bunny began.

"Oh, Bunny. You've always been too imaginative. You need to live here in the real world."

"I am talking about the real world, the mortal plane. Besides, what do you think happens to us after we die?"

"I go to church, you know."

"So, heaven and hell and all that? But what if you die unsatisfied and you're given the chance to speak again, to resolve something?"

"That sounds a lot like the silly Ouija board I got Alice for Christmas last year. She thinks she can ask questions of the beyond too."

"Well, maybe she can."

The sisters sat together in Bunny's dining room, eating their omelets, and avoiding any further uncomfortable conversation. However, the large lump they each had in their throats, that they had to swallow down along with their eggs, was twenty years of shared questions for one unsatisfied spirit in particular.

"Alice is having a bit of trouble in school," Rose broke the silence.

"Oh?"

"Yes, she's not very good at arithmetic. Though I suppose it's not abundantly important that a girl be good at math."

"If she gets married, she'll have to do all the household shopping and keep the accounting in order."

"If she doesn't marry *well*," Rose emphasized. "I am thinking about sending her to boarding school next year. Maybe the same one we went to."

"I hated that place."

"The nuns weren't so bad."

"No, it wasn't about the nuns."

Bunny rose to put their plates in the sink. She looked out the kitchen window again, but everything was still and silent.

"It's time to let all of it go," Rose half-shouted at her. "Hell, it was time to let it go fifteen years ago. You spent all your time at school mooning about and reading poetry to trees, or whatever you were doing, that's why you hated it. You simply refused to make friends. Bunny, you can't bring her back and you can't spend all your time chasing ghosts."

"I don't want to bring her back, I just want to know why she did it."

"It was an accident."

"I don't think it was."

There, she'd finally said it. Bunny shuddered with the relief of the unburdening.

"What do you mean?"

"I mean, I think she did it on purpose."

"You think our god-fearing Catholic mother committed suicide?"

"I think it's more complicated than an accidental drowning in a lake that she swam in often. She was a good swimmer, she taught us both."

Rose shook her head back and forth, "You just want it to be something else."

"Why would I want that?"

"Because it would add to your self-indulgent aura of mystery, it would make you more interesting."

"You think I'd make up our mother's suicide so I'd be more interesting at dinner parties?"

Rose shrugged. There was nothing left to say, no cards left tucked up anyone's sleeves.

"Well, I'd better clean this up. I have to go into the city this evening for one of those silly client dinners and I need to look my best."

"Bunny..."

"No, thank you. I don't need any help. You can see yourself out can't you?"

She stood gripping the countertop until she heard the door close, then she began to sob.

The phone rang again, much later in the evening, when Bunny had retired to her oversized clawfoot tub with a glass of wine and the phone nearby on a wooden chair she'd dragged in from her vanity. She assumed it was Rose looking to apologize and let it ring just a few extra times for good measure.

"Hello?"

"Bunny! It's Maria. How are you?"

Bunny looked down at her bubble-ensconced body, her turbaned head reflected back in the large suds in duplicate, triplicate.

"I'm just peachy. How can I help you?"

"I hadn't seen you at the library this week and I just wanted to make sure that everything was still good, that we were still on?"

"Of course, nothing's changed. I've simply been busy."

"What a relief! I was worried you'd changed your mind."

"Not at all."

In the background, Bunny heard a noise from Maria's end of the line. She took a brief moment to admire her new friend's imagined home, she felt Maria would be drawn to eclectic pieces of art, bright colors, layered rugs and tapestries. She imagined it was richly decked out, tasteful, less ostentatious perhaps than Bunny's wallpaper and star covered ceiling. She imagined Maria was the sort of person who had several houseplants.

"Sorry, my cat wants attention."

"Oh, you have a cat? How darling. What's its name?"

"Yes, she's a stray tabby I found as a kitten hiding out behind the library. I named her Lucky."

"Perfect. I have a parakeet, actually."

"They probably wouldn't get along."

"Probably not." She looked through the open bathroom door at the bird clinging to his perch in her bedroom, the occasional scuffling sound, the only other living thing in her house. He is an awfully quiet parakeet, I must bore him too, Bunny thought.

"I shouldn't keep you. I'm sure you've got dinner and things to do for your husband and kids."

Bunny chortled, the wine loosening her throat. "No husband tonight, no kids ever."

"I'm sorry, I didn't mean..."

"It's okay. No one ever means anything by it. But there it is, all the same. I wanted them once, I think. Kids, you know? I don't anymore. I think, I wanted him too. Same outcome, though."

Maria didn't respond.

"I guess it doesn't matter. He's off somewhere else and I am alone."

"I'm here," Maria offered.

"That's true, thank you for calling. I feel like a real person again. I think I will finish this bath and that book I have saved on my nightstand."

"Suppose I call again tomorrow?"

"Suppose you do. Goodnight, Maria."

"Night."

Bunny set the receiver down in its cradle and felt a little nauseous at having overshared like that with a woman who was more or less a complete stranger. She wondered also if Maria would in fact call again tomorrow, it gave her something to look forward to.

She took the parakeet out of his cage and let him sit on her shoulder, then her head, as she made a small green salad for her dinner. She let him clean her plate.

The housekeeper came early, so Bunny busied herself the next morning with a trip to the grocery store. She always ordered two of everything at the meat counter, two salmon fillets, two sirloin steaks, even when she wasn't sure when her husband would be home again. Once, she'd been caught by a club acquaintance buying only one salmon fillet and the look of pity that crossed her face resolved Bunny to never make that mistake again.

At home, she froze the steaks and went out to the garage to put another bottle of white wine in the refrigerator. She walked idly through her home, observing it as one might a museum. What sort of creature would live here? Why, it's the modern housewife! Alone, eating her single piece of fish, she cuts a tragic figure, but in the company of her husband, she's a glowing accessory. She has an associate degree in liberal arts, but the real achievement is that ring on her finger and all her fine things.

Bunny put on a record and lay on her chaise lounge with a magazine. Rose hadn't called, neither had Maria, and the day felt strangely empty though she was used to being alone. Perhaps anticipation inevitably led to exhaustion, though she couldn't remember that ever being the case before.

She stepped outside to smoke and sat down in one of the rocking chairs on her porch. Her husband did not like the rocking chairs, he wouldn't allow them on the front porch, but Bunny installed them out back and he never complained. They reminded her of her parent's house, her father sitting for hours staring out at the vast nothingness, her mother bringing him lemonade. Bunny sat in the chair, her toes on the wooden deck, nudging herself back and forth. She tried to recall if her parents had ever kissed, ever said 'I love you,' but she couldn't. She'd never felt there was a lack of love, but what did she know about any of that.

The neighbor woman was in the backyard again, hanging her underthings on the clothesline. Her bras were ample and caught the wind creating frothy white peaks of cotton and lace. Her slips were a variety of colors, black, nude, and white. Bunny imagined all of the occasions for such slips. Perhaps she still had a husband who took her out, or maybe she worked, volunteered. The woman went back inside to what Bunny imagined to be a cozy home.

I should work or volunteer, Bunny suddenly thought, before reassuring herself that offering to host a seance was certainly enough in the realm of volunteerism. "Join a church group," Rose kept nagging at her. This was good enough, better even, as she wouldn't have to leave her house.

The record player had stopped and was playing back that scratchy sound of emptiness, the whole house filled with it. She rose to flip the record to its B-side, when the phone rang. She didn't have the patience to wait and picked it up after the first ring.

"Hello?"

"Hello."

"Maria, I'm so glad you called."

"I wasn't sure if you really wanted me to."

"Of course I did. Let me pour a glass of wine, I want to hear about your day. Tell me something interesting."

Maria launched into a story about a library patron who kept trying to sneak his pet cat into the reading lounge despite being warned against bringing in pets multiple times. "People just won't listen," she lamented. Today, apparently, was the last straw when they found a cat turd under one of the tables.

"No!"

"Yes, I think he left it there deliberately."

Bunny burst into a torrent of laughter, "Maria, really!"

The women talked for an hour or so about nothing in particular, and everything in between, until Maria was called away by Lucky's need for dinner and Bunny to cook her solitary piece of salmon. She liked to use her cajun seasoning and cook the fish in ample amounts of butter, adding a squeeze of lemon at the end. As she ate her first bite, she found herself wondering what Maria would think of it rather than what her husband might.

Maria called the next night, and again the following. They related the high and low points of their days and talked about books they'd read, spiritualism, cults, why so many cars were gold, their favorite vacations, whatever happened to pop into their minds. For Bunny, it was the first time she'd had meaningful conversations with anyone since college and it felt good to have someone to check in with at the end of the day, to share your thoughts with and know they were listening.

For her part, Maria was a diligent landline companion and shared anecdotes about the library and Lucky. Eventually, Bunny stopped expecting the phone to ring with Rose and her apology on the other end, which was fine because it didn't come. Rose, immersed immediately into the world of her children's daily routine as soon as she left Bunny's, mostly forgot their conversation, adding it instead to her mind's locked vault filled with other instances she'd rather not recall. For Bunny, the phone came to only mean Maria, or possibly a dinner cancellation from her husband.

"I have so many boxes of this white wine in the garage," Bunny began one evening. "I thought I was ordering six bottles, but actually ordered six cases and, well, nobody likes it but me."

Maria chortled into the phone, "Six cases?"

"It was an accident!" Bunny insisted. "Still, it's Spanish, acidic and saline and everyone always complains that I don't have anything sweet. But I don't like sweet wine."

"Then you shouldn't buy it."

"Well, it doesn't do for hosting. I was thinking I may serve it at our event. Wine of any sort is often salubrious in a party atmosphere."

"I'm sure it will be appreciated."

"Have you spoken with Dr. Herbert?"

"Yes, everything is in order. He's already invited several interested members of his close knit group and, of course, you're welcome to invite anyone interested. We try to keep the gatherings small, six or seven people only, to keep from spooking the spirits."

"We might spook them?"

"They're not terribly keen on us in general. Sometimes it takes a lot of coaxing on our end."

"Understandable, I suppose."

Bunny briefly considered sending invitations around the neighborhood and really secure her reputation as a brooding eccentric.

"Time for Lucky's dinner, I got her a can of tuna fish for tonight."

"The lucky thing."

"I'll phone tomorrow and, obviously, we'll see each other next week."

"Next Friday."

"Yes, good night!"

Bunny hung up the receiver. The kitchen had grown dark in the time she'd spent on the phone. She considered cooking something for dinner, but instead uncorked the bottle of wine still in the fridge and turned on the television. Some late night show was on and a woman on screen in a sparkling fan girl getup was out hula-hooping the host who comically kept dropping his hoop. The audience hooted and cheered, Bunny lit a cigarette.

Her husband came home, then left again for his business trip. Bunny watched him pack his suitcase, an endless array of white shirts and satin ties, his golf shoes, a nonfiction book about the Civil War. She imagined him going up, up, up into the clouds, putting on his eye mask after the pretty air stewardess handed him a whiskey. She imagined the plane soaring through the sunrise, then suddenly plummeting downward in a mess of fire and panic, shrill voices screaming out for their loved ones. Who would he cry out for?

But that didn't happen, he called her from the hotel in California. Once the call confirmed he was as far away as could be, Bunny launched into preparations.

First, she had to pick the right outfit. Now, spirits were certainly dead, but would black be offensive, too funereal? She moved on to a deep purple dress she'd only worn a handful of times and flat black shoes. She added a string of pearls and, at the last moment, her turban hat. Forget what Rose thinks, she told herself.

She dragged the dining room table into the living room and rearranged the furniture to accommodate the large wooden thing. She moved the television to the garage, covered the table with a burgundy velvet table cloth, and set a silver chafing dish holding a collection of candles at the center, all different heights, some already burned. She arranged the chairs around the table and cushions on the floor, pulled the drapes to the dining room closed, and threw red fabric handkerchiefs over the lamps for mood lighting. She moved the parakeet's cage into her bedroom and covered it with a sheet, hopeful he would get the message and take a little nap.

Certainly the spirits wouldn't pass her by, Bunny thought, not with this cozy arrangement.

Food, she felt, was the next essential step. She whipped up deviled eggs, chicken salad sandwiches, with the crusts removed, and a crudité plate. The wine, of course, was also put on to chill.

At eight o'clock, Bunny lit the candles and watched them reflect back on the silver dish. The covered lamps emitted only the softest ruby glow. She put a jazz record on the player and poured herself a glass of wine.

At roughly eight fifteen, Bunny had finished her glass of wine and was anxiously picking at the edge of the table cloth.

At eight twenty, Maria knocked on the door.

"Bunny! I'm so glad to see you!"

The two women embraced. Maria was clad head to toe in a dramatic black dress that skimmed the floor and Bunny logged the information away for later seances. She noticed her friend also carried a large bag.

"Come in, come in. Can I get you some wine?"

"Is it white and acidic?"

"It is."

"Then yes, of course."

Another knock at the door sent Bunny skittering back to the threshold, admitting a series of people she vaguely recognized from the night of the lecture and a couple she didn't recognize at all. Dr. Herbert brought up the rear.

"Bunny, dearest, this is quite the setup!"

"I wanted it to be cozy for... for whomever may show up."

"Very thoughtful of you."

Bunny brought out the wine bottles and glasses, she placed her appetizers along the fireplace's mantle where people could congregate out of the way while Maria and Dr. Herbert set up. Maria placed a pendulum on the table, as well as a small bowl holding a bone. Bunny thought it best not to ask questions and instead tried to hold a conversation with some of the participants.

"Have you ever attended an event like this with Dr. Herbert before?" she asked one woman in a horrid multicolor crocheted skirt. When she whirled around to face Bunny, the scent of patchouli wafted about her in a perfumed aura.

"Yes, I have! Dr. Herbert has really helped me contend with the demons of my past."

"Oh?" Bunny leaned in closer.

"At the last conjuring, I was finally able to say goodbye to Putney." The woman dabbed at her eyes as though she might cry and Bunny realized she didn't have any tissues at the ready. How much crying did the typical seance induce, she wondered.

"Putney?"

"Yes he died tragically, in a hit and run."

"Oh my!"

"Of course, my parents, the heartless people that they are, immediately replaced him with a Dalmatian. As though Putney was replaceable!" The woman sniffled.

"Putney was... a dog?"

"Not just a dog! My closest childhood companion, my best friend... so loyal, so soft." Now she was crying and Bunny rushed to the powder room to fetch her a Kleenex.

"Oh, thank you," she dapped at her eyes again. "Dear

Putney! But I did get the chance to say goodbye thanks to Dr. Herbert."

Bunny nodded sympathetically and, tears stanched, she began to take her leave. A man in a beret and funny mustache took the woman by the arm and led her to the chaise lounge where she launched into another story of the loyal Putney.

Another woman stood by the door, she hadn't taken off her jacket and looked decidedly uncomfortable. Bunny walked over with the intention of drawing her in.

"Hello, would you like some food?"

"Does the chicken salad have walnuts?"

"No, it doesn't. Just celery."

"I don't like walnuts. They look like brains."

Bunny considered the two-halved nut and couldn't disagree. The woman entered the room fully and took a sandwich from the fireplace. She nibbled at it like a squirrel, her large teeth taking only the smallest bites.

"So, you're one of Dr. Herbert's fans?" the woman asked.

"I've only heard him speak once, but he was very engaging."

"He is. But you can't trust him."

Bunny widened her eyes in surprise.

"He's a charlatan, a snake oil salesman," she continued. "All pomp, no circumstance, if you catch my meaning."

"Why are you here then?"

"Oh, I'm here to do my own research."

The woman finished her sandwich and extended her pointed pink tongue to lap at her fingertips.

"If you'll just excuse me for a moment," Bunny mumbled.

She walked quickly from the living room, past Maria, into the kitchen where she leaned against the countertop to catch her breath which was coming in strange hiccuping gulps. Out of habit, she peered across the lawn into her neighbor's house in search of some comforting domestic scene, but it was shut up and dark. All these people in her house, what had she been thinking? Rose was right, *I am desperate and lonely.*

She reached into the cabinet and poured the already opened wine into an old jelly jar, all of her more appropriate glasses had now been commandeered by strangers. When she took the first sip, her lip on the ridged rim, she remembered again the fireflies and answered her own question.

Back in the living room, curtains closed behind her again, people congregated quietly and Maria had taken a seat at the table. She caught Bunny's eye and smiled at her. Wine-warmed, and less shaky now, Bunny smiled back.

"I believe we're ready to begin," Dr. Herbert announced.

Someone turned off the hall lights and the small group settled into the artfully curated gloom of Bunny's living room.

Bunny sat nearest to Maria, she felt safer close to someone who knew her. She wasn't certain if any of these others even knew it was her own house they'd invaded.

The woman in the crochet looked fidgety, she kept smoothing her hands over her skirt and looking over her shoulder as though she'd forgotten something important. Bunny watched a small brown moth flitting against the covered lamp in search of a false sun.

"We'll begin with an opening incantation," Maria announced, her husky voice breaking the awkward silence. There were no more sandwiches and wine to occupy their hands.

"Heavenly Goddess, we ask for protection from evil. Let nothing but light and goodness enter this home. Let only the blessed spirits pass over the threshold. Oh Goddess, surround us with your embrace of pure light and banish the darkness."

Vaguely, Bunny wondered which goddess they were praying to. Of course, she knew the Greek deities, the ladies of Mount Olympus and the priestesses who worshipped them. Was Maria a priestess of Hekate? Of Athena? Were they about to enter into the embrace of Penelope's shroud?

"We invite you spirits, leave your insubstantial world and reenter ours. My body is a temple for your unfinished tasks, your unrealized dreams. Enter safely, we will receive you with grace."

Dr. Herbert had closed his eyes and nodded along with Maria's incantations. When she'd finished, Maria held out her arms, palms up, Bunny resisted the urge to look at her lifeline. Her eyes were closed, as were many of the participants, Bunny could hear their rasping breath. Only one person met her eyes, the woman who was there to conduct 'research.' Bunny quickly looked away, back to her friend who appeared to be on the verge of some sort of rapture. Suddenly, Maria gasped and grabbed the side of the table, pitching her body forward. She was dangerously close to the candles, Bunny thought.

"There's a spirit here," Maria whispered. "A woman, older."

Bunny shuddered.

"A lover."

She calmed herself, but the older man at the end of the table had turned his wet eyes toward Maria's figure.

"She's such a calming presence, there's a smell like baking bread."

The old man was nodding now.

"Always fresh soda bread on Sundays," Maria intoned.

She paused and cast her eyes toward the ceiling, they all followed her gaze, except Dr. Herbert who still had his eyes closed.

"Of course, I'll tell him."

She met the eyes of the old man directly now.

"Your glasses are in the wardrobe, behind the penny jar, she wanted you to know."

Tears were streaming from his eyes, diverting through the wrinkles in his wizened cheeks. "That's just like her. Isn't that just like her," he whispered to himself and Bunny felt herself momentarily moved.

"Roses. Bring roses next time," Maria murmured before letting her breath out in a whoosh. "She's gone."

Another of the older participants was patting the old man's shoulders as he had begun weeping openly now. Maria said nothing, only resumed her position of supplication to the goddess. Everyone else waited, breathing only a little, a sip of air was all they dared.

Bunny remembered her mother's admonition, "Always hold your breath when you pass a graveyard lest the angry spirits get lodged in your throat." Touch wood for luck and wear silver for protection, always carry the St. Agnes prayer card, she protects little girls, she'll keep you safe. She and Rose followed these arbitrary rules without question, even now St. Agnes often marked her place in a book.

Maria's eyes began to roll and her breath came in fast, rasping gasps. It sounded a bit like an asthma attack, Bunny thought.

"Majorca," she cried out. "He's still in Majorca."

The researcher was staring hard at Maria, her piercing little eyes penetrating the distance between them like hot needles through ice.

"He was waiting, waiting, wasting. The drink, the drink," Maria moaned. "Like poison."

The researcher's face softened, Bunny could see her pink tongue again housed inside the soft 'o' of her mouth.

"There is nothing to do in a place so beautiful but wait and drink, what a waste." Maria's head whipped toward the woman who doubted Dr. Herbert and asked, "Why didn't you come back?"

"I—" she began. Her mouth pursed closed and she stood, quite unsteadily, backed away from the motley assembly, and left the house altogether.

She'd never taken off her coat, Bunny noticed. Dr. Herbert opened his eyes only briefly to watch her go. He leaned behind the enraptured Maria and whispered to Bunny, "This happens sometimes. It can be too much for those of a weaker constitution." Bunny thought it wise to just agree with him.

"He's gone," Maria announced, seemingly unperturbed by the quick exit.

The people gathered around the table looked frightened now, as though something had crossed the boundaries of propriety, these ghosts coming in without knocking, without announcing themselves first.

Maria's open palms almost touched Bunny's shoulders and Bunny thought, what if I were just to rest my head in her hand for a moment? Her desire to be touched, to be comforted, welled up inside her like a stone.

"I always loved to swim," Maria said suddenly.

Bunny looked straight ahead, daring not to look at Maria's head thrown back, the whites of her eyes showing.

"Water, water everywhere. That's how it was, quiet, peaceful."

Bunny stopped breathing, held it in her chest, precious breath. If only her mother had come up for breath.

"It was peaceful, I promise. I'm sorry, hunny bunny, I just didn't see another way to go about it."

Bunny looked at her friend now, Maria was staring back at her with her blank eyes. She touched Bunny's face with the back of her hand.

"It was oil or water. I had to choose," she whispered.

"But what about me?" Bunny whispered back, her voice hoarse with the effort of keeping the stone down inside her.

"I knew you'd be just fine. You are just fine."

The sob she let loose wracked her ribcage, shattered her chest. It was the sob she'd been holding since she'd left for boarding school, since Rose had told her to stop acting like a baby, since her father refused to speak of their mother ever again.

"She's gone," Maria whispered. Her eyes were shining again and looking at Bunny with such tenderness that Bunny started to cry again.

Maria resumed her position for what felt like ages. Bunny and the old man still quietly sniffling and trying not to make eye contact with anyone. Finally, she looked at Dr. Herbert and gave a little head shake.

"It appears the spirits have ceased to come among us this evening," Dr. Herbert announced.

"What about my dear Putney? Is he near?"

"Diane, you know we can't force spirits to emerge. Putney may have said his bit and now he's at peace. You want him to be at peace, don't you Diane?"

Diane nodded and began smoothing her skirt again.

Bunny's own mind swirled with the wildness of the experience, the raw emotion that had traversed time and crossed into her sitting room. Adrenaline buzzed in her blood and she felt her hands tremble with it.

Maria folded her own hands in prayer and placed them against her breastbone. "Goddess," she intoned, "through you we command all spirits, energies, entities in this place to return back to their own plane. Cleanse this home with the purest love and light."

Dr. Herbert passed Maria a clump of sage, she lit it and left it to smolder in the small bowl that had previously held the bone. Bunny tried not to wonder where the bone had gone.

People began to rise alongside the smoke, to join up in a small clump and follow Dr. Herbert toward the door where they congregated briefly before being sent out into the unfriendly night, questions still unanswered. Bunny envied them. She stacked their dishes and glasses and carried them to the kitchen like a ghost.

She stared at the jelly jar she'd earlier filled with wine, from a different lifetime. She stared at the mess in her sink and contemplated donning her rubber gloves, only their maid would arrive in the morning. What was the point? She had no purpose.

Bunny's eyes welled up with tears again and just as they began to stream down her face, utterly ruining her carefully applied makeup, she felt a hand on her shoulder. Maria, she knew.

"Are you okay?"

She wiped at her eyes, "Well, I'm not sure I'd go that far."

"It can be jarring, the first time."

"How did you know about my mother? I never told you."

Maria raised her eyebrows, "I know you never told me."

"So, how did you know?"

"I told you, the spirits speak through me. I am the medium."

Bunny shook her head, "No, that's impossible. That other woman, the one who left her lover in Spain, she told me Dr. Herbert was a charlatan."

"Well, he is a little bit. He tries to give an academic veneer to something that is purely spiritual. Spiritualism is hard for men like him to believe so he wants to make it scientific. He doesn't understand this is my inheritance, what my mother passed down to me, the ability to commune with spirits."

"Do you ever speak to your mother?"

Maria smiled, "My mother is alive, she lives in Aguascalientes. So yes, but on the phone."

"Oh."

"Bunny, I'm sorry, but the spirit who spoke to you wanted to break through. I felt her first, but I didn't know she'd come for you. She was insistent and when I finally capitulated, her power drove the others waiting back into the void."

"Yes, that sounds like her," Bunny agreed.

"Do you want me to help with the dishes?" Maria offered.

"No, it's fine. Would you like to meet my parakeet?"

Maria smiled and nodded. Bunny went into her bedroom and brought out the cage. She lifted the dark sheet and the bird's eyes opened as if to a brand new world. He began to chirp happily. Bunny pushed a piece of lettuce through the gaps in the wire and motioned for Maria to do the same. They watched the bird chirp and eat.

"Did Dr. Herbert leave?"

"He did," she paused, "I think he's sleeping with Diane."

"The crochet skirt woman?"

"Yes."

"Well, I never. How on earth can he compete with Putney?"

Then Bunny began to laugh, her girlish giggles set off the parakeet who in turn set off Maria and soon the two of them were doubled over in mirth clutching leaves of lettuce.

"Oh, Lord," Bunny wiped her eyes again, she had stopped considering her makeup at all. "Let's finish this wine."

She pulled another jelly jar out of the cabinet and filled both hers and Maria's. She lit a cigarette and offered Maria one, but she declined.

"I imagine you're pretty exhausted."

"The spirits are usually gentle with me."

Bunny smoked and leaned against the edge of her formica countertop. This house, everything so carefully chosen, she smirked. No one had even noticed she'd used the best wine glasses this evening, the lipstick stains and greasy fingerprints mocked her from the bottom of the sink.

"Listen," Maria began. "I am thinking about going to Mexico City for a while. My family owns a house there and I want to open a little shop, maybe a bookstore with a side of tarot reading."

"That sounds delightful."

"Their yard has all these fruit trees, avocados so big you wouldn't believe! The landlord has a parrot that rides around on his shoulder."

"Like a pirate?"

"Just like."

"It sounds like a fairytale."

"Well, I was thinking you could come too."

"Where?"

"To Mexico, with me. Maybe not for forever, but for a

little while. You could get some sun on your cheeks and visit the floating market and try mezcal. I think it would be good for you."

"I don't think I could do that."

"Why not?"

"Well, there's just... the house."

"The house?"

"I couldn't leave the house."

Maria smirked, "So, not your husband then."

"Oh, yes. My husband. And Rose."

"Has she called you? Have either of them?"

The phone sat accusingly in its cradle. Bunny snuffed out her cigarette in the glass ashtray and shrugged.

"Alright. Well, I'm leaving in two weeks. We should at least get together before then."

"As long as you promise not to summon my mother."

Maria held up her hand, "I swear."

The two women embraced and Bunny walked her toward the door, handing her the bowl of charred sage as they walked past.

"Don't stay asleep in a dream world, Bunny. There's more out there," Maria added, before donning her coat and stepping out into the night.

Alone, aside from the parakeet and perhaps the spirits, Bunny walked back toward the kitchen. She debated opening another bottle of wine but determined it would be ill-advised so late in game. She looked at the number her husband had scrawled on the pad they kept nearby for messages. "FOR EMERGENCY ONLY" he'd written above it. Was loneliness an emergency?

She dialed the number and requested his room. The phone rang twice, a bleating, desperate sound. She imagined it pealing across his dark and empty room, but it was earlier there, maybe he wasn't even asleep.

A woman answered, "Hello?"

Bunny almost laughed, but it came out as a scoff.

"Hello?" The high-pitched voice of someone certainly younger, more pert than herself.

"Put him on," she commanded.

"Who is this?"

Her husband's voice rumbled in the background, angry she'd picked up the phone. Bunny sympathized, she too had picked up the phone at inopportune times before.

"Hello?" He said, his voice all at once familiar and distanced by the tinny long distance reception. She wondered if he thought she was room service with the bottle of wine he'd certainly ordered to impress her by now.

"Hello darling, I was just wondering if you were feeling lonely. However, I suppose I've answered my own question."

"Bunny..."

She let him wriggle on the hook and refused to supply an easy out like she normally did.

"Look," he said finally, firmly, as though she might turn away, "There's nothing going on here."

"There never is, my love. Is she the office's California secretary or the hotel's maid? Or, tell me, is she the one who leaves cheap perfume always lingering in your clothes? I've washed her out many times over. Tell me, does she know about me at all? Oh, it doesn't matter does it."

She waited for him to say something. Maybe if he denied it three times before the rooster crowed, she would let him back in. Instead, she lit another cigarette and listened to her husband's raspy breathing filling the space around the phone's electric crackling.

"Fine. When you come back, I'll be wanting a divorce."

Bunny slammed the receiver into the wall, wishing instead she could press her hands all the way through the drywall. She broke a dark red nail in the process, which seemed almost to be the most unfair thing of all. She'd only just painted them.

On second thought, she would open that other bottle of wine.

That night, dizzy and weightless in her gigantic bed for one, Bunny dreamed of water.

The next morning, as she'd forgotten to put on eye cream and brush her teeth, she woke with fuzzy teeth and smeared makeup feeling the best she'd felt in ages.

At first, she thought to call Rose, to tell her about the seance and their mother's ghostly presence. "Closure, Rose, I got closure," she wanted to shout at her sister, "I feel free!" The image of Rose's downturned mouth when Bunny had mentioned her palm reading book flashed back to her and she decided against it.

Buttery sunlight streamed into the kitchen and across the formica countertops and the black and white chessboard tiles that Bunny dipped into on tiptoe when, face washed and turban donned, she emerged to face the day. Her parakeet, still in the kitchen, chirruped good morning and she almost laughed, what a charming sound! "Have a piece of lettuce little tweety," she cooed, pressing a green leaf through the bars. She turned on the coffee pot and listened to the familiar sounds of a solitary morning, the sounds that punctuated each morning of her life.

Across the lawn, she saw her neighbor standing outside with her hair in curlers, her housedress buttoned up to her neck. She was smoking a cigarette. Bunny walked out onto the patio with her black coffee, the air felt damp and warm, like it often does before a storm. She raised her hand in greeting to the neighbor woman whose name she'd never bothered to ask. The woman looked up, waved back. Then something inside caught her attention and she turned toward the door, then disappeared into the great maw of her house, of her unsolitary life.

Bunny finished her coffee and stayed outside even when it began to sprinkle, fine drops of rain that clung to the windows and drifted down in slow motion estuaries.

She picked up the phone and dialed the only number that she could think of, the only person who might care.

"Good morning, darling. Yes, it's Bunny. Did I wake you? I'm sorry about that... well, yes I did give it some more thought... I agree, I think it might be just what I need. Only, well, can we leave right away? Yes, today."

She spent the rest of the morning packing her luggage, sorting through mementos that she found actually meant quite little to her after all. Why had she kept these dried flowers, this theater program? Her life packed quite easily into three large suitcases. At lunch, she took a break and ate bologna straight from the fridge, not bothering with mustard or bread.

The child across the way was playing in the yard and Bunny was seized by an impulse.

Moments later, she rang the neighbor's doorbell. It chimed and echoed in their great entryway. Bunny noted the blandness of the decor, the emptiness that invited echo. She felt she was making the right decision.

The woman with the curlers answered, "Oh, it's you."

"Yes, it is."

They smiled at one another like two women who may or may not have been part of some conspiracy.

"What have you got there?"

"Well, you see. I am going on quite a long trip and I was

wondering if your son would get some enjoyment out of my parakeet? I hate to leave him to his own devices and I don't suspect he would survive on his own, he hasn't got the skills."

"Hmm. Is he loud?"

"The opposite. He sleeps with this sheet over his head, like so, so it's easy to fool him into thinking it's bedtime."

"And what does he eat?"

"Vegetarian table scraps, lettuce, carrots, bird seed if you have it."

The woman didn't look convinced and Bunny momentarily panicked, she lifted the sheet and the parakeet trilled out a howdy-do welcome that summoned her son from the back of the house.

"Mommy, a bird!"

The mother smiled like an oozing cheese at her offspring, "It is, my dear. Would you like to have a bird?"

The child was already squatting and peering into the cage, the bird peered back. They seemed to understand one another completely.

"I like him," the child announced.

"Well, this lovely woman has brought him to you as a gift."

"For me?"

"Yes," Bunny murmured.

"What do you say?" his mother prompted.

"Thank you! Thank you!" the child cried.

The mother smiled at Bunny, proud that he had effectively displayed his proper upbringing, and took the cage gently from her outstretched arms. The lightness in her own arms felt suddenly too heavy to bear and she turned away, walking quickly back to her house, her ankles gleaming wet from the damp grass.

Bunny was sitting in her living room, what she

considered her personal masterpiece, the exemplar of her taste, when Maria's car arrived. She let her friend in and they embraced. Bunny's eyes filled up quickly with tears and she laughed, brushed them away, "We have to stop meeting when I am in such a state."

"I could see you sitting in the window when I pulled up. What were you thinking about?"

"How hard it's going to be to leave all of this."

"All of what?"

Bunny gestured at her house, the sparkling ceilings, the carefully arranged mantelpiece.

"These are only things, Bunny. You can recreate this part anywhere, it's this part you have to save," Maria pointed to her own heart. "Besides, you were the one who called me and asked to leave earlier."

Together, they carried her suitcases out to the car. Maria's cat slept in a carrier in the back along with her two much smaller suitcases.

"Ready?" she asked. Bunny nodded, and Maria steered the car in the direction of the border. When they hit the highway, Bunny threw her turban out the open window and let her hair fly freely in the wind.

When Rose did finally decide to call, she found the phone off the hook and the house locked up and dark, preserved like a museum. That is, until the woman with the cheap perfume moved in, in the wake of Bunny's departure. She pulled down the wallpaper, painted the walls beige, and blotted out the ceiling's galaxy. Constellations weren't her thing, she'd never gotten any answers from the stars, and she meant to keep it that way.

The divorce documents were airmailed to Mexico City where Bunny signed them from her terrace that overlooked a garden with an avocado tree. Bunny took the money she felt was owed to her, she let him keep the rest. When it was finally done, she went down to the bar on the busy street where she often met Maria and the bartender with his dark mustache served her a glass of tequila with ice. He clinked the rim of her glass with his own beer, then glanced up. Bunny followed his eyes to Maria's slim figure clad in an embroidered floor length dress and leather huarache sandals as she came to sit beside her. They ordered more tequila and Bunny threw back her head and laughed.

PART TWO

The realtor drove Jessica all over town in the back of her BMW sedan because Jessica refused to sit in the front. "Someone might see me," she explained. The realtor, one of those Texas women who believes 'the bigger the hair, the closer to God,' wore a cream jumpsuit with a sparkling belt and wedge heels that crunched dry leaves underfoot as she got out of the car to open the sedan's back door. Jessica hadn't asked her to do that part, but somehow the realtor already knew her role.

"I think you'll really like this one, sugar." She kept referring to Jessica as different saccharine endearments. "I feel like it has the right energy for you."

Jessica adjusted her oversized sunglasses and stepped out into the sunlight to join her exuberant guide. She wore towering black stilettos because she too believed height conveyed power.

The ranch house was all brick with white columns, very antebellum. The circular driveway reminded her of the entrance to someplace grand, Buckingham Palace, maybe. The trim was an uninspired beige, but Jessica appreciated that it blended into the rest of the neighborhood, a seamless addition to the existing patchwork.

"It's got those mid-century modern touches you've talked about wanting," the realtor continued. "Plus it's a traditional ranch style house, all one level."

The realtor opened the door and ushered Jessica in. She took in the archways, the windows, the fireplace, all beautifully traditional and well-maintained. The kitchen still had the avocado formica and yellowing linoleum squares so popular in the sixties.

"It needs some work."

"Just a little updating in the kitchen, some new carpet, but I think the rest of it is very tasteful."

Jessica didn't respond, but followed her into the dining room, the bedroom, the living area. The carpet was a worn down brown and there were spots where wallpaper had been pulled down and painted over, she could tell in the corners. Her own mother would never settle for finishings of that quality, but Jessica didn't actually mind it that much.

The yard expanded out from a large back porch, privacy hedges had been erected near the fence line to eliminate any potential contact with the neighbors, an addition Jessica appreciated.

"Why did the price drop so low?"

"Well, it's a silly reason really."

"Is something wrong with the foundation, the roof? I don't want to buy it and have the whole thing cave in on me while I'm sleeping."

"Oh no, no! Nothing like that."

Jessica peered over the top of her sunglasses.

"Alright, well, the woman who lived here before wasn't too popular in the neighborhood and people remember her still."

"I thought the woman who lived here just moved to Florida after her husband had a stroke?"

"No, no, not that woman, the one before her. She just up and disappeared one day and he came home with a new wife, like he'd gone to the store and picked up a replacement. My momma lived just down the street at the time, they all went to the same church. Well, when the first wife went... are you sure you want to know about all this local gossip?"

Jessica nodded.

"My momma said the woman trucked with the devil and this house, her house, was haunted by spirits. She claims they even had seances here in the early sixties. So, with anyone in the local community, it still has a bit of a sordid reputation that precedes it, you understand? The new wife never really fit in 'round here, and some people even believe the first one had a spell put on her. It's all hearsay and nonsense, of course."

The realtor seemed out of breath when she'd finished, but Jessica's curiosity was piqued. Owning a home with a reputation that might keep people away appealed to her particular needs and sensibilities and she looked around her with fresh eyes.

"I like the yard," Jessica commented.

The realtor's face lit up again, "It's a wonderful yard! Lots of room for a pool, or to expand."

They walked together through the house again, back to the front door that looked out over the crescent shaped drive and the realtor's shining BMW.

"I want it," Jessica announced just as they reached the threshold.

"Really?"

"Yes, it's perfect."

They didn't haggle, Jessica happily offered the already reduced asking price and immediately began to negotiate the retrieval of her belongings from a storage unit in Los Angeles. She was in possession of the keys within the week.

"Why on earth are you moving to Texas of all places?" Ferdy asked her weeks earlier as they lay entwined on his bed in the little studio apartment he refused to leave.

"Have you seen that show *Dallas*?" Jessica asked him, her eyes focused on the slowly rotating ceiling fan that hardly ever cooled the room.

"That show about all those rich white people fighting about ranches and oil and whatnot?"

"That's the one."

"I try to avoid things of that nature," Ferdy rolled off the bed and lit the rest of a joint they'd cast aside earlier. He held it in a clip and exhaled smoke into the ceiling fan's direct path, the smoke swirled around them like fog.

"It's not that I want to *be* the people in the show, but I want to imagine I could be."

"You already are rich and white," he pointed out.

"I want to eat steak and wear jeans and slap someone."

"You can do all of that in LA," he insisted.

"It's just not the same."

They got high and stopped discussing it, but Ferdy hadn't come to her goodbye party and she was still upset about his snub. He didn't understand her need to start over. She just didn't want to be famous anymore. She couldn't explain that Los Angeles had made her famous, that it would keep her famous, that the city was a beautiful trap. And she was on the verge of no longer being beautiful in it.

She wanted to walk past people who didn't recognize her. She wanted to walk past people she hadn't slept with (already comprising a considerable amount of the city). She didn't want people to tell her she looked like that actress, she reminded them of someone famous, that somehow she had become a diminished version of herself. Ferdy didn't care about that though, he liked her better famous.

When her things arrived, she realized it would take more than a studio apartment's worth of furniture to fill such an expansive home. Even with all of her things, the place looked very minimal, which Jessica didn't mind. She hung a framed Picasso print above the mantelpiece and arranged several brass candlesticks underneath, a collection her mother had given her. She moved her plush maroon sofa at an angle that faced both the window and the new television she'd purchased. Her bedroom had just a bed, nightstand, and dresser that contained her carefully partnered bra and panty sets. The kitchen she filled with her unmatched pots and pans and she was again reminded of all the things she had meant to buy. She hid the full liquor bottle in the cabinets and dragged a dilapidated looking lawn chair, left over from the previous owner, to the backyard's concrete patio where she lay in the sun and smoked.

At least Texas also had sun, she thought to herself. The previous owner had erected an immense pergola that hung over the extended porch area and the shadow lines striped down her body like a tigress. The intermittent shade and potential for an uneven tan annoyed her. What was the point of this stupid contraption anyway?

The immense hedges provided a hazy outline to the edges of her yard, though she felt no desire to explore them, to take ownership of the land. She didn't want to tend to anything, in fact, she longed to cultivate nothing at all. I want to give myself over to an overgrown lawn, Jessica thought.

A rustling in one of the hedges startled her, she lowered her large sunglasses and tried to peer across the lawn. It rustled again, louder now. Her bony derriere was lodged in between two of the plastic strips on the lawn chair and she panicked, managing to flip the whole thing over on the side. Dislodged, her first racing thought was, what if they had gotten photos?

From the hedge nearest her chair, a squirrel came

tentatively out onto her lawn to inspect the property's new possessor. Who was this strange angled woman, her face white as a sheet, sunglasses askew? Unimpressed, the creature sprang up onto the fence and took off running.

"I wish I had a BB gun," Jessica muttered, rubbing her thigh.

A house or two over apparently had a dog of some considerable size and volume, the booming bark was triggered by the squirrel's easy passage.

"Git 'em, girl," Jessica cheered.

The barking went on while she dragged the chair upright. She went inside and came back with two cushions and a towel which solved the problem of her getting stuck again. Eventually, the evening air became chilly and Jessica realized she had at least five angry, red mosquito bites on her pale legs. This place is already trying to eat me alive, she thought.

Inside the kitchen, the single AC unit buzzed noisily. She turned it off and listened to the distinct quiet of the Dallas suburbs. Her chest loosened and she remembered why she'd come here, in search of peace and quiet.

Jessica had a rented car, nothing to rival her realtor's BMW, but she decided to take it into town. She wanted to see what sort of nightlife the suburbs might possess. As it turned out, not much aside from an ice house with a metal bar and rough looking clientele. Jessica's hair was tied up, she wore only a little makeup, and blue jeans. It wasn't quite the *Dallas* disguise she'd intended, but it would do.

A football game was on the large television above the bar and no one looked up when she walked in. So far, so good, she encouraged herself.

The bartender, a bald man with blue eyes and a black t-shirt, approached her. He wiped down the bar in front of her with a scummy white towel, then asked, "What'll you have?"

Several choices floated into Jessica's mind: a dry gin martini with extra olives, a bottle of Prosecco, some snow. No, none of those would do.

"A beer?"

"What kind?"

"Um, your call."

The bartender rolled his eyes and popped the cap off a bottled pilsner.

"Thanks," she said, sliding two dollars in cash across the counter.

Jessica sipped the foamy head and grimaced, it was at once both bitter and flavorless. Still, it thrilled her to be doing something so utterly not-Jessica, or new-Jessica. If only Ferdy could see me now, she thought.

She turned slowly on her barstool to take in the rest of the unique establishment she now found herself in. Metal road signs and sports pennants hung on the wooden walls. Some of the road signs had bullet holes shot through them in collections of twos and threes, Jessica wondered if the damage had been done before or after the signs had come to adorn the bar. Half of the bar was exposed to the outdoors and people stood outside smoking and talking, looking every once in a while at the game inside. She wondered if the smoke might keep the mosquitoes at bay.

Something happened in the game and up and down the metal bar men shouted and fist pumped. "Fuck yeah, that'll show 'em!" The cresting wave of testosterone alarmed her for a moment, as though they might turn it on her. Instead, they mostly sloshed pale yellow beer onto the bartop and Jessica understood how the bartender's towel had gotten so scummy.

She didn't join in the festivities, but quietly picked at the label on her bottle, watching the easy interactions of people who belonged there.

Her guard down, she ordered a second beer. It tasted slightly better than the one before. She lit a cigarette and a man two barstools over pushed a glass ashtray toward her.

"Thanks," she mumbled, making an effort to keep her voice soft.

He nodded, then turned his attention back to the television and his friends.

Jessica ashed her cigarette and wondered if she should have taken that cheerleader part. They'd offered it to her a few years ago, the main love interest in a movie about a faded football star who came back to coach his old team. Back then, she was still the hot young thing, but she'd been insulted by the role. She wanted to do *serious* film, she still aspired to the stage. But, even after several fairly successful theatrical runs of independent plays that resulted in just enough fame to keep her relevant, she realized her Hollywood sex appeal had fizzled. The last casting she'd gone in for was someone's mother, those were the roles left to her now — she was Lady Macbeth.

She watched the glitzy Cowboys cheerleaders run out onto the field in their white daisy dukes and go-go boots. She watched them kick and smile with their gleaming white teeth. She watched the men at the bar all watching the same scene with stupid shit-eating grins on their faces. And she felt a pang, an errant thought: I wish they were looking at me.

As if on command, a woman appeared at her elbow. She was ordering a vodka and cranberry juice from the harried bartender who clearly did not want to turn away from the television's onslaught of sparkling white. Jessica glanced at her, only to make direct eye contact with the woman's curious gaze, she flicked her eyes away, then back again. The woman continued to stare.

The bartender returned with her drink, she ignored him. Jessica could feel it coming, she longed to get up and walk away, but that would look more suspicious.

"Excuse me," the woman began, her nasally Texas accent pressing against each word. "Excuse me, but aren't you...?"

Jessica turned to look at her, to make her finish the question. Let's see if she really knows who I am, she thought.

"You're an actress," the woman continued.

Jessica didn't help her.

"You were in..." the woman faltered.

"No, I think you're mistaking me for someone else." She turned her attention back to her beer.

"No, no, I recognize you."

"I have one of those faces."

"Shakespeare! I saw you in something with Shakespeare."

"I don't know the man."

The woman frowned, then took her drink back to her table where Jessica could peripherally see her gesticulating to her companions, her Barbie pink fingernails pointing toward the bar, drilling into the back of Jessica's head. She turned away but could feel the table collectively turn toward her. She'd paid her bill, she could leave, Jessica told herself. She put out her cigarette, stood, and walked toward the exit, past the groups of clustered smokers and the parallel parked pickup trucks.

Inside her car, she laid her forehead against the cool leather of her steering wheel for a moment, then turned the car toward home and left the bar behind, fully knowing that woman would tell anyone who would listen in their insular little suburban circle that she'd seen Jessica Fairchild at the dive bar. Hopefully no one would believe her.

At home, she realized the beer had done nothing for her state of mind, and she reached into her cabinets for the handle of vodka. She poured two fingers into a plastic cup, she used the searing liquid to chase her sleeping pill. She had gotten a six month supply before leaving Los Angeles and already she'd dipped into it. And besides, *how am I going to find such a willing pharmacist out here,* she wondered, before falling asleep.

She woke to the shrill insistence of the cordless phone she'd left by her bed when ordering pizza had still seemed a possible ending to her night. The alarm clock blinked 11:00 AM in an offensive red.

"Hullo," she rasped into the receiver, her tongue still felt thick with sleep.

"Hello, is this Miss Jessica Fairchild?"

The lilting voice, the false cheer, she felt immediately on guard.

"Who's this?"

"I'm Arnie Hampton with the *LA Times*, I've been trying to get in touch with you about an interview request I'd submitted a while back. You see, I want to talk about the natural progression of Hollywood, glamour to grande damme. And I finally found a new listing for you out in... Texas? Your agent isn't being incredibly forthcoming about any of this, but I do have a deadline and..."

"I'm sorry Arnie, but you've got the wrong number."

Jessica pressed the red phone icon and Arnie's intrusion was blissfully silenced. She flopped back on the pillows, her long limbs splayed out across the lilac bedspread she'd brought with her from California to this palace of regret.

The cordless phone still in her hand began to ring and flashed green with a Los Angeles zip code.

"Nope," Jessica cried out into the emptiness of her bedroom. She marched into the kitchen and pulled the cord out of the wall. She knew they'd keep coming like ants to a pot of honey. She'd never be rid of them. They'd insinuate themselves into the walls, crawling and swarming until she gave in. Her skin crawled with the invasion she sensed would soon be at her doorstep.

First, she needed to get her number unlisted. She plugged the phone back into the wall and immediately began to dial. They agreed to unlist her, but it was probably too late for the reporters. Once one finds you, the others follow like flies to a carcass.

Without much direction, Jessica wondered what she might do to occupy herself for the rest of the day. The vodka lay tantalizingly open, no one would know after all, she reasoned. She poured two fingers, no, three, with ice cubes and walked outside. The heat of the day felt oppressive, heavier somehow than Los Angeles, even with all its smog. She lay down on the lounge chair and let the sun crush her back down towards the earth, like a warm hand pressing on her chest.

After the second glass of vodka, she decided to try and see if she could still do the routine from her first off-Broadway musical, *Johnny Boy*. It involved a series of robust and acrobatic kicks. Jessica, wildly swinging her long legs through the air, more or less attempted to recreate the choreography. She hadn't actually been one of the chorus girls, but rather the main love interest, finally utilizing those singing lessons her mother had paid for. "You're a brilliant Soprano," they'd encouraged her. Too bad the play only ran for a few weeks before being relegated to obscurity.

"And kick, and kick, and kick," Jessica announced to no one, splashing the vodka over the rim of her glass. "One, two, three, onetwothree!" Until, legs akimbo, she fell ungracefully off the side of the raised patio and lay in the grass, dazed, staring up once again at the sun.

The days bled into one another and Jessica wondered how long she could simply stay in the house without leaving. She thought about the saints, the holy hermits, who withdrew entirely from society and subsisted solely on prayers and water. *I could do that, only I'd need to turn the water into wine and cigarettes,* she thought.

One morning, she opened the door to her circular driveway and rapidly growing lawn, already threatening to reclaim the territory once ceded to concrete. Next to her morning paper and *Life* magazine was a flyer announcing: "Jimmy's Lawn Mowing Service! He'll do it twice as good as anyone else." Below was a phone number and a jaunty drawing of a smiling lawn mower.

"Passive aggressive little shit," she mumbled. But, the lawn was looking raggedy and she certainly wasn't going to purchase a lawn mower herself.

She reconnected the phone once more and called the number. She made an appointment with his mother for him to come over the next day, Saturday, his mother expressly forbid working on the Lord's Sabbath.

"We wouldn't want him to come to any mortal harm," Jessica agreed sweetly, before hanging up the phone and lighting a cigarette. The exertion of talking to Christian mothers was more than she could bear. By now she'd realized the glamorous oil tycoons were more likely in

Houston and the best she might be able to do was slap the president of the local PTA.

Jimmy came over right at nine o'clock and knocked on her door, one two three. Jessica had her hair tied up in a kerchief, her big sunglasses and red lipstick on. She'd thrown on an oversized tank top, absently neglecting to add a bra, and neon purple bike shorts. She opened the door and Jimmy looked visibly taken aback.

"Hello, I'm Jessica."

"Jimmy." He was pale faced and freckled, his red hair like candy floss in the sun. He was the same height as her, and she was quite tall. She estimated that he was in high school, though still lanky as though he were an outline of a man, not fully filled in.

"Perfect. So, obviously the yard needs a little work, if you wouldn't mind. The backyard too, it's all flat. How much do you charge?"

"Five dollars, ma'am."

"Ma'am," she laughed. "Five dollars is too little, I'll give you ten if you do a thorough job."

Jimmy's eyes widened further and he set off like a firecracker. She shut the door to the sound of him cranking the ancient lawn mower to life. Hopefully that creaky old thing will make it through the whole yard, she thought.

The silence of the house felt less punishing knowing that she was showing initiative in its upkeep. She made a plate of egg whites and absently flicked through her magazine, painted her fingernails aubergine, and blew idly on them while she watched Jimmy toil through the backyard. I should make him some lemonade, she thought, before remembering she didn't have any lemonade. She didn't have any groceries at all. Ah yes, I'm a female hermit, she reminded herself.

Jessica walked out on the porch with a glass of ice water for her hardworking employee. He smiled gratefully and downed it all.

"Jimmy, I was wondering..."

"Yes?" His pale eyes beseeched her.

"Well, it's just that I haven't had any time to go grocery shopping since I moved in."

The boy nodded, sweat dripping off his delicate nose.

"Would you perhaps be willing to do some shopping for me as well? I can pay you extra."

"Anything for you, ma'am!"

"Well, I'll just write you up a list then," Jessica cried, gleeful at having solved her problem. "And let me just get you another glass of water."

She paused, then added, "Do you think they'll let you buy alcohol?"

The boy shrugged, "Sure, I do it for my dad all the time."

"Perfect."

Jimmy stored his lawn mower under the shade of the pergola and drank another glass of ice water before setting off with Jessica's list already crumpling in his sweaty palms, utterly disbelieving of his luck. Jessica, for her part, felt similarly.

She could hear the neighbor's dog barking again now that the lawnmower noise had calmed. Did that thing ever stop?

She walked back inside, shut the door, and lay back on the worn-in sofa to admire her fingernails until a knock at the front door jolted her upright. This time the knock was hard and fast, not tentative like Jimmy's. The boy couldn't be back already, could he? She tiptoed to the peep hole and peered out, but she certainly didn't recognize the man on the other side.

"Hello?" She called.

He looked up, "Yes ma'am. I'm here with a delivery."

"Delivery? Of what?"

"Flowers, ma'am."

"From who?"

"Well, I'm not allowed to open the letter…"

"Oh fine, hang on."

Jessica undid a series of four locks and deadbolts then opened the door to the delivery man who did indeed offer her a large vase filled with cut flowers.

"Thank you."

The man gave a polite nod then headed back to his van which was idling in her crescent drive.

She shut the door, dead bolted it again, and walked the flowers into the kitchen. The vase felt heavier and heavier the further she carried it into her house. Jessica's stomach turned over as she set the bouquet on the counter. She took a step back to examine it — anthuriums, birds of paradise, cascading jasmine, decorative palm fronds — it was bursting with tropical color and fragrant with life. Jessica hated it.

She opened the decadent red envelope and, in sloping cursive, it simply said: 'please reconsider, xx."

Annoyed, Jessica tossed the card on the counter. Of course Ferdy would send her this ostentatious peacocky display to make amends. "What a jerk," she muttered. But it only took a moment before she was dialing his number into her cordless phone. It rang twice before his sleeping voice came across the line.

"Hullo?"

"Ferdy, you absolute pest, how did you even find me in Texas?"

"Texas? Jessie is that you?"

"Of course it's me, and I got your silly bouquet. It's hideous."

"Bouquet? You're mistaking me for one of your admirers again."

"I just got it!" She cried.

"Well, it wasn't from me. I don't even have your address, remember?"

"Of course you don't, you threw me over."

"I threw *you* over, oh that's rich!"

"Well, here you have my number on your phone now."

"How is your little Southern backwater anyway?"

"Miserable. Hot. It's perfect."

"I'm so very pleased for you."

Someone knocked again at her door.

"I believe my errand boy is back, so I have to go. But... I do miss you, Ferdy."

"I miss you too, you selfish bitch."

She hung up the phone, smiling, and let Jimmy inside, his arms laden with all of her goods. He helped her put her groceries away and earned his money. The morning had become afternoon, and he explained he was going to be late to the Widow Gordon's house and would now be forced to mow her yard at extreme speed while she hurled obscenities at him from the window and then only paid half.

"So, thanks so much for the tip, ma'am."

"All this ma'am-ing, it makes me feel old! Call me Jessica, after all, we're friends aren't we?"

"Alright... J-Jessica," Jimmy stuttered, blushing. He'd never called an adult by their first name before.

She ushered him and his lawnmower back to the front porch, waved goodbye, and went to survey her wares. Jimmy had managed to get several cans of tuna fish and a box of saltines, bananas, eggs, coffee grounds, tomato juice, cigarettes, Tang mix, and a fairly hefty bottle of vodka. Good job, Jimmy, she commended his initiative.

Jessica opened one can of tuna and a sleeve of the saltines and decadently spread the mashed fish in oil across the top of a salted cracker. She chewed slowly, with the intention to make it last, and looked out at her lawn. It looked fairly evenly cut, he'd missed a few errant spots near the edges, but she didn't mind. All freshly shorn, the yard invited a barbecue party, or perhaps she needed to install an inground pool. A pool would really be the height of glamour, she thought.

A burst of color appeared in her peripheral and Jessica jumped at its intrusion. The flowers! If Ferdy hadn't sent them, then who on earth had? She moved the vase to the kitchen counter, loathe to throw away such a ridiculous bouquet. She had to admit, the riotous display of houseplants did capture her particular humor.

She finished the can of tuna fish and filled a glass with tomato juice, then, on second thought, she added vodka and ice. She walked barefoot to the kitchen and turned on the television, the news, anything to fill the empty sounds of the house. It was evening now and she listened to some nice man with a hairpiece tell her about the weather until it switched over to a game show and the white noise lulled her to sleep.

The phone rang early, she'd fallen asleep with the cordless receiver again and now it brayed out its urgent alarm with insistence. Her first thought was: my agent might be calling with a part! But the dim light of her living room dispelled her of that notion, he would never call before nine o'clock, and he wasn't calling these days anyway. Perhaps it's Ferdy, she considered, before ultimately pressing the green lit button.

"Hello?"

"Good morning Miss Fairchild."

"Who's this?" She hissed into the receiver.

"Arnie, Arnie Hampton. I hope you received my flowers."

"I knew they were a trap," she muttered.

"I read in an interview you liked Birds of Paradise."

"Of course, I gave myself away."

"I was actually wondering if you'd reconsider doing an interview with me."

"I wonder if you'd reconsider harassing me with early morning phone calls."

"I apologize for the earliness of the call, but I hoped to catch you before you went out. Usually it just rings and rings."

Jessica flopped back into her bed and sighed loudly.

"Anyway, you see, I've been doing some research into your earlier career."

Jessica sat back up and screwed her face into a grimace.

"The commercial work in New York, then LA... you worked with a Mr. Gregory Parker in your modeling days didn't you?"

"Thanks for calling, Arnie," Jessica hung up the phone and turned the ringer to silent.

She had goosebumps on her arms and knew that sleep was off the table, so she decided a morning bath would have to do. She carried in her stack of glossy magazines and set them on the toilet while she filled her claw foot tub. The tub's gold feet were certainly one of the lesser reasons she had settled on this house. It made her think of something out of a children's fairy tale, as though the tub might get up and walk off with her still in it like she were Baba Yaga in her chicken leg house.

The bathroom filled with a heavy curtain of steam and

she dumped a handful of pastel colored bath beads into the water. They sat, pearlescent, at the bottom until their coating was coaxed away by the warm water and they released an aromatic oil. It smelled like lavender and eucalyptus now and Jessica gingerly lowered her body into the tub. The water was almost too hot and her skin reddened immediately.

Her mother had always warned her not to sit in their hot tub for too long. "You'll boil your organs," she'd warned, but Jessica had always felt comforted by the warm water.

She held her magazines in her painted fingers, dangling slightly over the edge of the bathtub and read about people she might have thought of as her peers in Los Angeles.

"There's Macy in her pretty little dress, I always told her she should wear purple more," Jessica noted aloud to her audience of no one. "And look at Jason, his newest girlfriend is only twenty-one, I heard. Well, she'll find out about him soon enough. Rena is finally starting to look old." She looked down at her own naked body, then turned the page, "Oh, a quiz to see how sexy you are." The smell of the magazine's perfume samples mixed with the bath beads in a heady way as Jessica sat in the bath and took the quiz, she received an eight out of ten.

Her cordless phone blinked with '3 missed calls,' but she returned it to the charge station without checking who they were from. She hadn't set up an answering machine yet and didn't intend to. Arnie had rattled her nerves this morning and even the bath hadn't fully cleared her head.

Moist and lavender-scented, she began to weigh the pros and cons of a walk. What I need is some fresh air, she decided. What was the worst that could happen? Aside from paps hiding in her hedges, of course.

She put on her largest sunglasses, an oversized

sweatshirt, and a pair of jeans. I look like any inconspicuous suburban housewife, she assured herself. Then, with much effort, she propelled her body out into the still cool morning.

She stood on the porch surveying the front yard, the hedges, the cars parked nearby. Anyone could be lurking. Just then, someone walked in front of her driveway and Jessica made to duck, but it was her neighbor with Walkman headphones on. She waved to Jessica, then set off again. Jessica walked out onto the sidewalk and followed in the Walkman woman's wake.

The houses here were all different, not like the area she'd grown up in where the houses were pre-fabricated and cheap looking. Some of these were designed by famous architects, people Jessica had actually heard of before. Her own house was small in comparison to some of the others. She wondered again about which of them might have a pool.

After walking a block or so, she heard the familiar barking of the neighbor's dog. The yard in front of their luxurious brick mansion was fenced in with an ornate iron gate. The dog, a fluffy white thing, barely bigger than one of Jessica's handbags, came flying down the drive, flinging itself toward the fence and barking like a mad thing.

"Well, you're not as intimidating as you sound, you're just a little creampuff."

The dog sat and looked at her, panting a little, worn out by his own blustering.

Jessica squatted and stuck her hand out for him to sniff, which he did, then she scratched behind his ears and he panted back at her.

"You're not all bad are you, you just need a little attention. I get it."

She stood to continue her walk and the small dog sat, pressed against the fence, watching her go. Jessica felt the familiar pang of leaving someone behind.

She passed several more yards, each landscaped in the same bland way, dew drying slowly on the rows of monkey grass that reached over to tickle her ankles. A little further on, a man walked out onto his front drive to collect the paper and waved in Jessica's direction. She waved back this time as though they were friends. More than friends, neighbors, she told herself.

Back at the house, she felt more relaxed, focused. The sun cut horizontally through her blinds and enticed her back outside. I need a project, Jessica decided. The garage was filled with discarded tools, the limited essence of a man who no longer was. What need did the previous inhabitant have of these items at her condominium complex in Florida? They'd stayed behind. Now, Jessica dug through the detritus, some of it quite old, then walked out to the backyard armed with some metal screws and a battery powered drill. She began to reattach the plastic strips on her aging pair of sun lounge chairs. Sitting cross legged on the ground, she pulled each alternating white and blue strip taught, then attached a rather crooked screw underneath. It was a loud and sweaty project she immediately regretted undertaking, but, at the end, she surveyed her achievements through the small kitchen window and drank a cold glass of water feeling quite satisfied with herself.

The sun dipped low behind the hedges and Jessica replaced the water in her glass with ice and vodka. She deserved it, after all. She carried a few throw pillows outside and lay down on the sun lounger that still lingered in a slice of late afternoon sun.

She dozed off and woke some time later, the sun was

gone now and her body was imprinted with the thick lines of her newly strengthened sun lounger which had pressed its own length against hers. In the distance, near the hedges, something sparkled like twinkle lights in the purple darkness. Fireflies, she realized. Against the backdrop of the looming hedges, the small insects blinked on and off like so many stars.

Having successfully forgotten about Arnie in the expanse of the afternoon, Jessica walked back inside her house and went to bed feeling capable and relaxed.

The days blurred together. She played solitaire at the kitchen table, watched MTV, and stayed up too late watching the Home Shopping Network and stirring vodka into her Tang. She ordered lingerie from a catalog that was accidentally sent to her address. Some days she didn't wash her hair, a ritual she'd adhered to since her teenage years, and enjoyed the feeling of breaking a routine. Sometimes the phone rang, but she let it echo through her sparsely furnished house, and turned up the TV as a countermeasure.

One day, she picked up the phone, ready to tell Arnie where to shove his interview. "Now you listen here, you stop calling me!" She shouted into the receiver.

"I'm sorry, Miss," came a small voice.

"Wait, who is this?"

"It's... it's Jimmy."

"Jimmy, darling, I'm so sorry. I thought you were someone else entirely."

"I just wanted to see if you wanted your grass cut again. It's been a while, only it's getting colder now, so I thought you might not."

Jessica looked out the window, the grass had indeed

grown again to a weedy height. She hadn't noticed and felt tenderly thankful for this young boy looking out for her.

"Of course. Would you like to come by on Saturday morning? Oh, and could you come early? I have a little shopping for you, if you have the time."

"Sure thing," he sounded excited at the prospect of the shopping. "I'll be there at seven sharp."

Jessica almost interjected to say she hadn't meant *that* early, but decided not to crush his enthusiastic spirit.

"See you then, Jimmy."

"Bye Miss!"

"Jessica," she corrected.

"Miss Jessica."

She hung up the phone feeling very benevolent, like a nun, someone who gives herself over to helping others. Jimmy would make a cool twenty bucks in addition to his mowing money and she would get her fridge restocked as a bonus. She sighed happily at the prospect of avoiding the supermarket again. The last time she'd almost frozen in the meat aisle, paralyzed by the choice of cuts, the endless array of pink flesh before her. It made her feel dizzy, sick. In the end, she'd panicked and bought several fillets of catfish, which she had no idea how to cook. Luckily, the butcher had offered her blackened and lemon pepper as flavor profiles, so it hadn't been a complete disaster. Still, the idea of Jimmy doing that for her made her feel infinitely more relaxed.

On Saturday, Jessica rose early and put on a large t-shirt and jeans, her hair in soft rollers. She opened the door to Jimmy's rosy face at exactly seven, just as he said.

"You're punctual, sir."

"It's my guarantee," the boy replied seriously.

She smiled and said, "Front yard and back, you don't need to be too fussy about it."

"I always do my best."

She half expected him to salute her, but he simply turned on his heels and pulled the cord on the lawn mower, roaring it into life. Jessica watched him make linear passes over the grass. She admired the stylistic approach and was reminded of her own mother running the vacuum over the carpet in precisely spaced stripes.

Jessica took the rollers out of her hair and tousled it into loose waves that fell to her shoulders like trails of ivy. Although low on supplies, she cut some Spam into thick slices and toasted two pieces of white bread that she smeared with margarine. She offered it all up on a paper plate like some kind of sacrament, assuming the boy would need a snack.

Jimmy and his lawn mower eventually moved to the backyard and the droning sound became meditative. She put MTV on silent and listened while she walked in circles, trailing her fingers over the countertops, wondering who might have had their hands there before. She envisioned a woman, young and eager, wearing yellow cleaning gloves. She imagined her dropping a spoon, bending over, her husband looking up from the television, the two of them going to bed in the same room Jessica slept in now. Would the woman look up at the ceiling as stars exploded behind her eyes? Or would the husband turn back to the television, annoyed at her clumsy interruption?

Her reverie was interrupted by a sweat soaked Jimmy standing in the doorway. His face seemed more freckled than she remembered it, or perhaps it was simply more eager.

"That was record time," Jessica exclaimed.

"You don't have much to go around, it's real flat."

"Isn't everything here flat?"

She nudged the plate toward him and he put two slices of Spam on top of a toast slice. Jessica made a note that he appeared to be eating with gusto and could repeat the snack in the future.

"Well, sure," he nodded, chewing, "But like, old Mr. Whitacre's house has all these overgrown rose bushes. He won't let me touch 'em, so I just go around. It takes forever."

Jessica nodded back, imagining her neighbor's yard crowded with creeping tea roses. Pink, red, and, she supposed, yellow since they were in Texas, after all.

"Your yard, it's a big blank square and I can just jog across it."

"Should I get some rose bushes?"

Jimmy screwed up his face, "They're an awful lot of work. And Mr. Whitacre always has scratches on his arms. Could be from his cat though."

"Maybe I'll plant something on the porch, just so you don't think I'm too boring."

Jimmy's eyes widened, "I don't think you're boring at all."

Jessica laughed, a throaty sound, perfected from her acting days. "Still, maybe I'll get a cactus or something."

Jimmy nodded again. He had finished all the Spam and toast and a large glass of ice water. Jessica took the plates to the sink and he lingered awkwardly by the counter, not knowing what to do next, or how to ask. She let him squirm for a minute, remembering her own inclusion into the world of adults and their conversations. He still wasn't quite sure when it was appropriate to cut in.

"Well, are you sure you don't mind going to the grocery store again for me? I know it's a lot of work."

"Nah, it's nothing. Only a few blocks over."

"I got you some canvas bags so you don't have to worry about the paper ones breaking."

"I'll look like a dork," Jimmy protested. "Only the old ladies use those."

"Well, your arms won't be so bogged down. See, you can carry them," she demonstrated.

"Fine," he huffed, allowing the bags to be hooked to his arms.

She tucked a list and some cash into one of the bags and wished him well on his journey.

Once the boy was walking down the street, Jessica turned the sound back up on her TV. They were re-airing a performance. Blondie was on stage singing, her hair bleached and wild, she wore a leopard top and her nails were painted black.

The memory came back of attending a concert in New York, rolling her body against a sea of other bodies, trying to make contact with one person in particular. Greg had been her studio theater teacher in an old community theater downtown, he showed her how to project her voice, to inspire confidence when she walked into a room, and, in the downtime between auditions, he helped her get modeling gigs.

Once, when she was on a shoot and nervous, Greg leaned in and whispered in her ear, "You're so goddamn beautiful, you're capable of anything." Her eyes widened, grew moist with emotion, and she looked up toward him with unguarded emotion.

"Now," Greg commanded the photographer, who took a series of shots.

Later, when she saw the image spread out on the table in his apartment, she could hardly believe the glistening eyes, the flushed face, the bee stung lips, were her own.

Greg smiled his panther grin and said, "It's pure sex. I knew you had it in you."

That was the first night they slept together, a passionate and naive coupling that Jessica neither regretted nor romanticized. He was married to an art dealer and she was one of several ingenues. She became a model of moderate renown, got her first movie part as "Girl #3," and they kept sleeping together until they both got bored.

Curse Arnie for bringing all this up again! Only, she knew Arnie wasn't interested in talking to her about a decades old love affair. No, she felt certain he knew far more than he was letting on. There was only one reason a reporter would go digging in her past for Greg.

When Jimmy returned, she slipped out of her simmering rage as though it were a negligee and smiled at him.

"Truly enterprising! Did you find it all?"

"Yeah, I got it."

"Even...?" She prompted.

"I got the vodka, but the guy said my mom might like cranberry juice better than Tang, so he gave me both. Hope that's okay."

"Of course, thank you." She paused. Like Greg, she often had an urge to smash something beautiful. "Have you ever had a drink before?"

"Just a sip of my parent's beer, they don't really drink."

"Christian?"

"Mom's a strict Baptist, but she pretends she doesn't see dad's beer in the garage fridge."

"Sounds like my parents." She didn't tell him the part about how they'd probably divorce as soon as he'd left for college. "Do you want to try some?"

"Uh..."

"No pressure," she added, turning back to smile at him as she opened the bottle over the sink.

He firmed up his face and said, "Sure."

Jessica put ice cubes in two highball glasses and two fingers of vodka, then she stirred in a little cranberry juice, enough to make it opaque.

She held out the glass to Jimmy, "Here ya go. Is it too strong?"

He took a sip, "It's not bad."

"C'mon, let's watch TV."

They sat down on opposite ends of Jessica's sofa and watched music video after music video, until Jimmy started giggling at a Dorito's commercial.

"What's so funny?"

"I don't know." His face was flushed pink and she noticed his drink was gone, the ice melted down into a faded pink remnant.

"Do you feel alright?"

She scooted toward him. The commercial wasn't funny at all, she wanted to tell him, you're just in that delightful place before things go dark. She surveyed his face. His eyes were wide, doe-eyed, and she knew she had the power to whisper to him too, but there was no reason, no photographer, no end game. She didn't feel any passion, just a little bit of guilt.

"You'd better get going before your mom calls over here."

"Oh shit, if I'm not home for lunch she'll go on a tear, that's for sure."

"Do you want to keep your lawn mower here?"

"Is that alright? I can get it tomorrow after church."

"Sure thing."

He stood hurriedly and brushed his pants several times as though they were dirty. "Uh, thanks, this was fun," he added before rushing out the door and into the too bright afternoon.

Jessica tidied up and poured herself another vodka and cranberry. In the distance the creampuff dog barked and barked. She opened the window so she could listen to his lament.

"We're both very lonely," she told the empty kitchen, and threw back the entire glass letting purplish juice leak out of the corners of her mouth.

That night, Jessica dreamed she was covered in hundreds of spiders like a second skin. The looming bodies of Daddy Long Legs created shadows on the walls of her bedroom. "You know, they're the most venomous spiders, but they can't bite you," her mother's voice told her. Somewhere a baby was crying, Jessica felt certain the baby was her, that her mother needed to save her from the spiders. In the space between sleep and waking, she swung her arms wildly into the darkness, upending a lamp and the glass of water she'd placed by her bed. Her heart beat against her ribcage and she rolled over, shivering.

Hours later, Sunday morning blazed rudely through her window and Jessica pulled a silk clad pillow over her head to keep the daylight out.

The phone began to ring at half past nine, the cordless was on the charger next to her bed. She contemplated throwing it across the room, but recognized the local area code and picked up, thinking it could only be Jimmy coming to get his lawn mower.

"Hello?" She rasped.

"Of course you're not up yet, not even out of bed are you?" A woman's shrill voice rang down the line.

"Excuse me?"

"Jimmy said you went to church, but I knew he was lying. Another sin!"

Oh, Jimmy's mother, she realized fuzzily.

"My son had a roaring headache this morning and had conveniently forgotten his father's lawnmower at your house, is that right?"

"It's here, yes." Jessica sat up straighter in bed.

"An excuse, no doubt, to return to your den of iniquity! Do you know he told me his head hurt so badly he couldn't go to church?"

Jessica didn't say anything.

"I know a thing or two about hangovers..."

Jessica thought about the father's beer fridge everyone pretended not to see.

"And I could swear that's what he was suffering from this morning."

"Maybe he just didn't feel good."

"Now don't go defending him! He came back from your house all flushed and glassy eyed, ate more than his share of lunch, and then went to take a nap that he didn't wake up from until this morning."

"He worked very diligently over here."

"He's coming back over to get the lawn mower this morning, I'm sending his father with him, and I want you to stay away from him."

Jessica considered how the father might be interested in a drink from her kitchen as well.

"You hear me?" The woman shouted. "You just stay away from him, you...you hussy!"

The phone line went dead and Jessica lay back in her bed. She felt oddly calm, a little disappointed that her *Dallas* moment had been somewhat anticlimactic. She had been hoping for a showdown at the country club, a gin and tonic spilled down the back of someone's dress. The wet meat sound of flesh on flesh.

She went to the kitchen and took two ibuprofen with a large glass of water, mentally she toasted to Jimmy and his headache. She put a piece of white bread in the toaster, then spread a thin layer of orange marmalade on it. She leaned over the sink and watched the crumbs fall toward the drain like a fine layer of sawdust. When she'd finished, she stood sucking the soft bread out of her teeth and surveying her hedges, filled this morning with a small grouping of finches. Twitchy little things, Jessica thought, as she watched them hop from branch to branch, just like everyone else here.

At half past ten, she heard a truck pull up into her circular drive. She tightened the sash of her bathrobe and tiptoed to the front window like a burglar in her own house. She opened the blinds just enough to watch Jimmy's paunchy father help him load the lawn mower into the truck bed. Jimmy looked appropriately miserable and Jessica felt a pang of guilt. He turned mournfully toward the house as his father climbed back into the driver's side.

Jessica pulled the string on the blinds, exposing her wild hair and stolen robe in the gaps, Jimmy's eyes snapped to the window. She raised a hand in farewell. Jimmy smiled and waved back. She pulled the blinds closed and watched the truck turn at the stop sign, leaving the street desolate once more. At least until the dog started up again.

In the bright morning light Jessica noticed for the first time a layer of grime on the carpet. She could see where her footprints had worn a path from the kitchen to the sofa to the bedroom, dust bunnies gathering along the baseboards like tumbleweeds. For a moment she considered cleaning, then remembered she didn't have a vacuum or broom or dustpan. Maybe I should call someone to come clean, she thought, before settling down onto the couch with the TV Guide. Considering how things had gone with Jimmy, she thought it might be better to simply ignore it all.

She wanted to smoke a cigarette and ash it on the floor, to make an even more elaborate mess. Her enduring contribution to the arts would be garbage, she'd throw everything away, reduce it all to dust. The cigarettes were hidden in the microwave, where she'd stashed them after she'd gone through a pack in one afternoon. She turned on the TV and watched the weather channel, a storm was rolling in across the west.

The phone rang again and Jessica realized her living room had turned dark orange in the late afternoon light. Somehow an entire day had passed. She'd finally gotten up for the cigarettes, only to find she'd actually hidden them inside an old cereal box, she was too smart for her own good sometimes. Presently, she ashed one into an empty beer bottle, dropped the butt inside to sizzle in the warm backwash, then laid her arms across her chest like a corpse.

She answered the phone, half hoping it was Jimmy's mom come to yell at her again, to make her feel less distant from herself. Yes, I am here, I am a bad person.

"Hello?"

"Jessica, so glad I caught you."

"Hi Arnie."

"Have you given any more thought to an exclusive interview?"

"I can't say that I have."

She muted the TV and watched the weather patterns swirl forward and backward into themselves, melding together, emerging as something else.

"I feel like you should know, I found her."

"Found who, Arnie?"

"Your daughter."

Jessica sat up slowly, lifting herself through the invisible fog and back to the surface.

"Sorry?"

"I found your daughter... the one you gave up."

She placed her hands on her stomach, soft now but still mostly fla t, perhaps grown slightly rounder since she'd left Los Angeles. But she remembered how it felt to have the skin pulled taut like a drum, using both hands to rub coconut butter into her skin, praying she wouldn't end up with stretch marks. She did get them, of course, but they were faded now like silvery fis h swimming up the skin of her lower abdomen.

Greg had paid for her to stay in a cottage in upstate New York once she'd started to show.

"Don't get too comfortable," he warned.

But she made herself right at home. In the mornings, she did yoga stretches with a VHS tape and made cups of warm water with lemon and honey that she drank outside on the small deck. It was miles to the store, but she had the use of a car, and enjoyed driving along the winding roads. On weekends, when he could get away, Greg visited, but he refused to touch her now, as though she were a loaded weapon.

He had been furious when she realized she was pregnant. Her strict modeling diet had halted her period for months and now it was too late to have an abortion. They hadn't even been sleeping together in the most recent weeks.

"What the hell are we going to do?" Greg raged.

Jessica, younger and calmer, simply replied, "We'll give it up for adoption. I don't want a child, Greg. I'm just starting my acting career. I'll disappear for three months, tell my agent I needed some country air, whatever, and I'll come back fresh and free."

Greg calmed down, he petted her hair, kissed her forehead. "Yes, yes, that's what we'll do. I have a place upstate, Claire has shows booked for the rest of the year so we won't use it."

She winced at the use of his wife's name. Then, of course, when Jessica did come back, she didn't feel free at all. Los Angeles was the first place she'd run away to.

"I don't know what you're talking about, Arnie."

"Sure you do. Don't bullshit a bullshitter. She was Greg's, wasn't she?"

Jessica didn't respond.

"I understand, it was still the sixties and he was married."

She breathed into the phone.

"But did you give her up because of the deformity?"

"The what?" She croaked.

"Her legs, the deformity in her legs."

"I... Arnie, I truly don't know what you're talking about."

"Oh, come on! Your daughter was born without functioning legs. Her adoptive mother said she looked like a little frog, knees turned outward, unmoving. You can't have not noticed."

The birth was brutal. Hazy from the anesthesia and utterly alone, Greg was at a gallery opening in the city and couldn't come, the doctor said words like, "complications" and "breech." She swam underneath the current of the drugs and disappeared. When she awoke again, the nurse's concerned face peering into her own alarmed her.

"What?" Jessica rasped. "Can I get some water?"

The woman handed her a cup with a straw and Jessica sucked at it through dry lips as the nurse paged her doctor.

He sat next to her bed and matter of factly explained she'd had some complications, "placental abruption," they'd had to remove her uterus to control the bleeding. She wouldn't be able to have any more children. At the time, she was just glad to be alive, nothing else mattered, she had a movie part in eight weeks and she asked how long it would take to heal, she had a life to get back to.

"I only saw her for a moment," Jessica whispered to Arnie, "She was bundled up like a tiny football in a pink blanket. She was beautiful, but I refused to hold her, I didn't want to get attached and I feared my own hormones would send me all haywire. They took my womb too, did you know that part? But I never saw her again."

It was Arnie's turn to be silent.

"The church organized the adoption, it was supposed to be private, though I guess that didn't work out."

She lit another cigarette and inhaled deeply. It burned, but not enough. She wanted to be scarred.

"It makes a good story, Arnie, I'll give you that. Ice bitch ex-actress abandons special needs love child she had with married man – it's real good."

He sighed, she heard it through the receiver as though he were sitting in the room with her.

"It is a good story, but maybe it's not the right one to tell."

"No, maybe it's not."

"Jessica?"

"Mm?"

"I'm sorry."

"That's alright, Arnie. By the way, I did like the flowers. Thank you."

"You're welcome. Oh..."

"Yes?"

"She's fine, by the way. Her family is very loving and

supportive, she's an accomplished flautist and she is beautiful, just like you said."

Somehow that was the worst part of the conversation and Jessica sucked in her breath. Her abdomen ached like a bruise.

"Goodbye, Arnie."

The line went dead and Jessica wiped at her cheeks, she was crying.

"Fuck!" She yelled into the empty house. "Fuck, FUCK!"

It took another cigarette and two more beers for her to calm down. Her heartbeat still thudded in her ears and she desperately wanted some weed, something to settle her stomach and calm her nerves. She'd even laugh at a Dorito's commercial. Of course, there's no where to get grass in this godforsaken place, she thought, no Ferdy, no semi-reliable friends to help a girl out.

Well, she had one friend. She dialed Jimmy's phone number.

He picked up on the first ring, "I knew you'd call."

"Just pretend you're talking to someone else. Look, I need a favor."

"Sure."

"Do you know anyone who can get me some weed?"

"Like… a drug dealer?" He whispered.

"Or just a friend."

"My cousin always has dope, I can call him."

"Thanks Jimmy. And, hey, I'm sorry."

"It's okay."

They hung up and Jessica's head began to throb. She poured what was left of the vodka into a glass and laid back to await whatever fate had planned for her. She half expected the cops, or Jimmy's irate mother, but an hour later there was a quick staccato knock at her door and, when she finally got up to open it, a McDonald's bag sitting on her porch.

She looked around, no one was out, no police cars, no sirens, it was dark and the streetlights had come on like in some Victorian novel, only she'd missed the lamplighters. No police cars, no sirens.

Inside the bag was a quarter pounder with cheese, fries, and a very small plastic baggie of weed. Enough for one joint, she figured. Her heart rose up unbidden into her throat, she felt incredibly cared for in that moment. The plant itself didn't produce much of a smell and she imagined it rolled up in some college boy's sock drawer growing more and more stale, until she'd asked for it. She found a discarded chewing gum paper and put the weed inside, rolled it, her saliva coinciding with the sticky gum residue to seal the whole thing tightly, then lay back to smoke and eat the still warm fast food. Reality faded further into the distance, and she floated above the ground again. Exactly where I belong, Jessica told herself, above all of this.

She fell asleep with the joint smoldering in her fingertips. Later, she woke in the night to smoke, real smoke, the kind that reminded her of campfires when she was a kid, or when she and Greg spent the night on the beach in each other's arms, throwing sticks into a blazing pit to keep warm. The memory was almost a fond one, she almost drifted back to sleep to dream fuzzy dreams about sparks by the ocean.

Wait, she sat up and sniffed at the air. Someone told her once that if you smelled burned toast it meant you were having a stroke, was this a stroke? No, this smelled worse. She saw smoke curling around her like a Medieval mist.

Panic coursed through her, she rushed to the nearest window and threw it open to the night, seconds before her sofa began to burn. For the first time, she was thankful to be in a ranch house rather than a sixth floor penthouse, and climbed out onto her lawn. From her new vantage point she could see smoke rising up into the night.

She held the cordless phone in her hand despite not remembering she had grabbed it. She dialed 9-1-1.

The firetrucks were there in moments, another benefit of living in a suburb where nothing much happened. The EMTs herded her into the back of their ambulance, they shone a penlight in her eyes, asked if she could breathe, did she need oxygen. "I'm fine, I'm fine," she kept repeating. They wrapped her in a blanket and left her there. All the neighbors came outside to congregate and speculate. They all had their theories of course, a single woman living alone in a cursed house, she was lucky she hadn't met her own untimely end. "Bad luck," they all agreed.

"It's mostly just smoke damage," the firefighter told her after they'd contained the small blaze. "But you got out just in time, the sofa was immolated."

Jessica nodded, chastened by her own bad behavior.

A flashbulb caught her attention and Jessica knew she was no longer anonymous. Minor celebrity burns house down, the paps would have a field day. The firefighters chased away whoever it was, off to sell her to the highest bidder.

Down the street, over the din, Jessica could hear the creampuff dog barking, could just make out his small ghostly figure jumping against the fence. It felt comforting to know someone cared.

The firefighters lingered to supervise her packing a bag, they called a hotel and a cab service, and only dispersed once they'd seen her safely off. They didn't see her circle back around the block for one last thing she deemed essential.

She checked into a downtown hotel that night, a nice one with the fluffy bathrobes she liked. She got fully undressed, turned on the hot water in the jacuzzi tub, then used the hotel phone to call the number she'd copied down into her little address book. It rang twice.

"Hullo?" The deep voice was muddled with sleep.

"Hello Arnie, it's Jessica."

"Oh." She could hear him rustling around in the darkness, grabbing a pen, his glasses. She felt certain he wore glasses. "What is it?"

"I just wanted you to know I burned down my house."

"You what?"

"I burned down my house, well, not entirely, but certainly a little bit."

"Are you okay?"

"I'm fine, at a hotel for the night. Here's the thing, someone took my picture. I imagine it was one of yours, or someone adjacent, maybe a pap on the move. But anyway, there's this picture out there and I wanted you to know first."

"Uh huh."

"You see, I was thinking, it might be a better story. Maybe this could be a good trade."

"I think it could."

"I'm at the Dallas Hilton in the honeymoon suite if you need me. But if the photo's not too unflattering, you can just go ahead and run with it."

He was out of bed now, she imagined, rubbing his eyes and wondering who to call.

"Okay, yeah. Talk soon, then."

They hung up.

It was around four in the morning and she stepped into the bubble bath and let the smoke seep out of her pores and into the lavender water. The bathroom had a small television mounted above the toilet and a phone underneath. Jessica reached for it, her arms steaming, and dialed 1 for their 24-hour room service.

"Yes, I'd like a bottle of champagne, or whatever you have that's sparkling, sent to my room. Yes... Prosecco is fine. Oh, and a hamburger patty. No, no bun or anything. Okay thanks."

She turned on the weather channel and sank back into the bath. It looked like the swirling Western storm had finally cleared and there were only reports of sunshine in the days ahead.

She turned on the jacuzzi bubbles and marinated until room service knocked at the door. She answered, wrapped up in the robe and still slightly damp and pink. A man in all white wheeled in a silver cart with a bottle of Prosecco, a metal tub filled with ice, and a hamburger patty on a white ceramic plate.

"Would you like me to open it for you?"

"That would be lovely."

He did an admirable job of quietly disgorging the cork and pouring her a glass. He quietly removed the second glass back to the cart and made to leave. Jessica placed a twenty dollar bill in his hand and he disappeared back into the hallway.

She walked over to the king sized bed bedecked in pristine white linens with her glass and the hamburger patty. She tucked her legs up under herself and burrowed into the pillows.

"Hey, I got you a snack," she said, placing the plate on the white bedspread where a powder puff dog lay curled up around himself. He wagged his tail and licked Jessica's hand in greeting, then set to work on the hamburger patty. "See, there isn't much to bark about anymore is there?" They watched the Home Shopping Network side by side, then the morning talk shows, before finally falling asleep.

Her agent called the following day both furious and triumphant. She was on the cover of the entertainment rags, they were making her out to be a tragic heroine, an aging Hollywood starlet, forced into hiding by the fast-moving LA scene.

"Some writer gave you a five paragraph write up, listing all your accolades and most recent theater reviews — Arnie Hardy, or something, he's done you nothing but favors. Even the picture of you sitting in the back of the paddy wagon isn't bad. The smeared makeup looks almost ghost-girl chic. Look, I've got people calling from all over, you have to get back here before this publicity disappears, poof! Let's make some appointments for next week. You're infamous, baby!"

Jessica heard herself agreeing — yes, she could get on a plane tomorrow, no, she didn't have anything to wrap up here, yes, I'll see you soon.

When she called Ferdy, he answered with a droll, "I already saw."

"I'm coming back."

"I knew you would."

When she called the real estate agent to put her house back on the market, the woman sighed heavily and cried, "Not again!"

Jessica boarded the plane from DFW to LAX with her dog, re-christened Snowflake, and a single carry-on, leaving the rest of it behind.

PART THREE

Amanda connected her ring light to her laptop, angled it just so, then logged into Zoom and stared at the blank white screen: 'the host will let you in soon.' She swallowed the nerves in her throat and sipped her glass of infused lemon water.

The screen lit up and she recognized the blonde and bubbly host of *Get Inside: Modern Apartment Living* immediately. Amanda religiously watched her interior design webseries on YouTube, often attempting to emulate the same artistic sensibilities for her own Instagram following.

"Alright everyone, welcome to *Flipside*! You've all been hand selected from hundreds of other applicants to join us for this new season of house flipping mayhem! As you know, each of you will be flipping an entire home for the competition, but there can only be one winner! The winner will get three hundred thousand dollars and will be a spokesperson for *Flipside* over the next year."

The host clapped and the muted thumbnails of the other contestants silently clapped alongside her. Amanda was half listening, half sizing up her competition in the sidebar. One thumbnail contained a couple, both cheerfully smiling into the camera, another had brought all their kids onto the call, another couple, an awkward foursome squeezed in together, couple, couple, then there was Amanda. She assured herself that she was the most well-lit at least.

"Since you're all in different parts of the country, we'll have an assigned crew for each flipping team. I know you already signed the contracts, but just a reminder that you'll be sharing the space with us whenever necessary. You'll also have a personal camera for filming your video journal, checking in each day about how things are going."

Amanda had been practicing her vlogging voice and trying to find the right approach to her video diaries. She knew from watching previous seasons of the show that they spliced this footage in after a particularly difficult day or used it for extra content online, behind the scenes stuff. It was important to come across as relatable and knowledgable, especially as a female contestant. The men had it easier, they could don a flannel shirt, swing a sledgehammer around, and get thousands of likes. The women had to be pretty, personable, and able to competently wield a power tool.

The host continued, "Finally, we'll fly the winner out to our studio at the end for the big finale. Now, there should be a surprise arriving at your houses soon!"

On cue, Amanda's doorbell rang.

"Go on," the host encouraged them. And everyone rose in tandem to answer their separate doors, their squares sat abandoned and the host quickly checked her teeth in the camera.

On Amanda's porch was a medium-sized red cardboard box. She carried it back to the kitchen where she had her laptop set up facing the pale pink wall of the dining area, the only presentable part of the house at the moment. They'd been asked to treat the flip house as though they were living in it, it needed to look lived in, they were repeatedly told. By now, the other thumbnail people had begun to open their boxes so she did the same. Inside was a lot of Flipside swag, a hat, a water bottle, then the hand camera the host had mentioned, and a brand name drill which several people were holding up triumphantly, their celebrations still on mute.

"Great! It looks like everyone got their package. There are some instructions for your camera, make sure you read those, filming starts Monday. Otherwise, I'm looking forward to speaking with you all again soon!"

Amanda could see some of the silent thumbnail people raising their hands inside their squares, wanting to ask questions, or make some comment, perhaps just say thank you, but they were frozen in their plaintive position as the host ended the meeting for everyone.

Amanda let out a whoosh of air. She'd been holding her breath mostly to suck in her chin on camera, but also because the house had a backed up sewer issue and smelled pretty awful. It was the first thing she'd called someone in to do on Monday.

She'd used part of the trust fund from her parents and all of her life coaching earnings from the last year to purchase this run down house for less than one hundred thousand dollars. It was located in an unpopular Dallas neighborhood that was originally all set for large scale demolition, only the project got postponed several times and, after a prolonged fight with the city, the development group had ultimately decided to liquidate the houses at a loss.

Amanda had been watching online real estate listings for a while and, when these houses began to pop up, she recognized the one she wanted immediately — the one Jessica Fairchild had lit on fire. She'd just watched a docu-series called *Broadway Broads* and Jessica had been featured as one of their actresses of note.

They'd shown a recent interview with her, her white hair in a chic bob, hands covered in silver rings.

"And what about all that mess down in Texas?"

"An ill-advised detour. One I was careful not to repeat. I really learned 'don't mess with Texas' the hard way."

The host laughs and Jessica smiles primly.

It was a quick aside in a longer interview, but Amanda had done some light Googling and found the original articles about the fire. It hadn't been a large fire, but it *had* happened in the living room in which she now found herself. Amanda was determined to add a historical glam to her design makeover, and she had a sneaking suspicion she'd been chosen for Flipside in part because of the house she'd managed to acquire. It came with a pre-fabricated story, they didn't need to work as hard.

Her boyfriend had been less enthusiastic about the venture. He worked for a tech company as a project manager and thought she could be doing something more useful with her time, her money. But Amanda was dead set on proceeding with the project and, when she'd received the acceptance letter, he'd begrudgingly opened a nice bottle of wine to celebrate.

She just had the weekend to mentally prepare and she made a mental list of all the things she still needed to do, including getting her eyebrows and nails done before the first filming day. Amanda loaded the box and her laptop into her Prius and drove across town to the condo she shared with her boyfriend in a chic new development.

The place smelled slightly of vinegar and something else sickly sweet which made her recoil when she opened the door.

"David, what are you making?"

She headed into the kitchen, which was empty, except for a pile of pots and pans in the sink.

"David?"

He stuck his head out of the bathroom, "I'm deep in the fermentation process, Amanda. I need to concentrate."

"You need some concentrate?" She half-heartedly joked.

He rolled his eyes at her and disappeared back inside where he often jettisoned their bathtub as a fermentation tank for his various vegetable and occasional beer experiments. Luckily, they had another half bath attached to the kitchen where she could escape to pee without the overwhelming smell.

Amanda cracked one of the living room windows to let the place air out. The windows were the type you couldn't open all the way for safety reasons and the hinges stopped her, allowing just a few inches of fresh air. The condo looked mostly neat she noted, their complex provided weekly housekeeping as part of the monthly fees. David had been insistent on the appearance of cleanliness, though the pots and pans belied his own efforts.

"Is a housekeeper really necessary, it's just the two of us," Amanda had asked, the price causing her a bit of pause.

"Well I know you aren't going to do it," he'd snarked.

It was true, she hated cleaning.

She'd wrapped up at the house fairly late, everything for the show happened in Pacific time, and it was past dinner. She looked through the fridge for something to eat. David also ordered pre-packaged meals from a local vegetarian health store. He'd been on a health kick in the last year, since finishing grad school. Well, they both had, it was an offshoot of her life coaching brand. After Amanda had taken some courses, she'd tried the methods out on David since he always complained that, working in tech, he felt a competitive need to keep trim. "No one wears anything over a size medium, and most people get their clothes tailored in the European style," he'd explained.

She'd wanted to be supportive since she felt slightly responsible for how far he'd taken her light suggestion of 'eat more vegetables,' so Amanda was mostly a vegetarian now.

Though she'd always been mostly ambivalent about food, she did use the change to promote her life coaching brand. "Plant-powered," she added to her Instagram bio with a little leaf emoji. She didn't tell David that sometimes she ate pork tacos from a street stall when she could no longer contemplate returning home to another of his limp salads.

Feeling frustrated by the labeled and orderly stacks in the fridge, she opened a green juice and made a bag of microwave popcorn. She was settling in to eat and watch a re-run of Flipside when David finally emerged, his hands covered in something red and sticky that looked as though he'd just finished a surgery shift or a day at the butcher shop.

"Oh my god, are you okay?" Amanda asked.

"It's just beet juice, don't be so dramatic. Is that what you're having for dinner?"

She nodded and turned the TV up, listened to him carefully prepping every minute aspect of his dinner, which she knew was tofu and quinoa based on the remaining fridge stacks.

The host who had spoken to Amanda via Zoom only an hour prior, now appeared before her in full HD resolution. She walked the audience through a tour of one of the homes before Flipside got involved. "There's only one way to describe this space — unloved! But watch what can happen when someone is willing to get their hands dirty and give this space the attention it deserves." Through a time lapse video, the host showed all the differences the contestants had made in the kitchen particularly. At the end, a smiling couple stood staring back out at them looking accomplished.

"It seems so fake," David complained.

"Well, it's not. You should know that by now."

"I know it's not, but c'mon. She's very, you know, shiny."

"She's shiny in real life too."

"Oh, right! You got to meet everyone today. How did it go?" He settled in and looked at her expectantly.

"It went great! The host was so sweet and accommodating. I'm really excited to start. The only thing…"

"Yes?"

"Well, the other contestants were all coupled up. I was the only single-appearing one there."

"You're not single though."

"I know, but if you're not involved at all it makes me look a little pathetic."

"I told you this was your project, you wanted to take it on. I wanted to go to Burning Man. We agreed on that, remember?"

"I know."

They sat in silence letting the blue glow of their large, wall mounted television wash over them.

Amanda scrolled through the photos she had taken of the house that day and settled on one of the backyard, she added a filter and pumped up the saturation, made it look lush and verdant rather than overgrown. She posted it to her Instagram story with an added caption, 'Can't wait to get started! Catch me on the #Flipside!'

She licked the popcorn salt off her fingers and leaned back against their sofa.

"What are you doing?" she asked David, who was clearly looking at his phone.

"Checking crypto prices. I really want to invest in GollumCoin."

"Like the Lord of the Rings character?"

"Yeah, it's the hottest new crypto. A lot of the guys on my team are rolling their entire 401k accounts into some crypto or other. What do you think?"

"Roll your entire retirement account into GollumCoin? No, I don't think that's wise."

He looked a little pouty and glanced back down to his phone.

"I mean, I don't really know anything about crypto, so you do whatever you think is best."

"I just don't want to miss out on a good opportunity."

"Sure, like I did with the house. I get it."

"And you don't know much about remodeling houses either."

He was right, she'd worked as the office manager at a real estate office for a few years in college and while she helped support him through grad school before creating her online brand. She'd watched these women, girl boss types teetering in expensive heels, make hand over fist cash. She'd convinced a few of them to take her out to the interior design appointments, paid attention to what was popular, expressed interest and admiration. Everyone always told her she had an eye for color, an eye for what worked in a space.

Toward the end of her sojourn there, the real estate office held a social media focused competition called DreamSpaces that Amanda had entered. Each participant redesigned a space in someone else's home and people on Instagram voted for which ones they liked the best.

Amanda chose a new mother's nursery. The mother had twins and Amanda knew the mother wouldn't have any time to work on the room herself and would appreciate almost anything, but she went with an ethereal cloud theme, even sponge painting a soft cloudscape on the ceiling. She added a mobile of birds and kept everything a cool color scheme. She made sure the furniture was multi-use and functional as well as aesthetically appealing. She hung opaque, spherical lamps above a silent rocking chair and added a wall mounted book shelf filled with donated books both for mother and child.

The office had filmed the mother crying in thanks, but even without that Amanda won handily, her online prowess also allowing her to to promote herself to a larger audience and eventually leave the real estate office to work for herself.

Again, she rolled this experience into her life coaching brand, 'Feng Shui friendly' with a sparkle emoji.

"I think I've found a good plumber to come in Monday at least."

"Is he cheap? You think you can stick to the one hundred thousand dollar budget?"

"He said he'd do it in part for the TV exposure. I guess he's already been on HGTV and it got him a lot of new business."

"That's smart. You have to work the connections, the benefits."

"Kind of like being an influencer, it's all for the exposure."

David nodded, he'd switched the TV to a soccer match. It was the new thing at his office, to eschew American football for 'the real football.'

Amanda scrolled through the responses to her Instagram story: "Get it girl!" "You've got this!" "Bring Texas the trophy!" And a lot of heart and fire emojis. She smiled, people got it. She'd post some behind the scenes stuff and make sure to simultaneously share her upcoming 'Heart

& Home' workbook about making your home an extension of your heart. She'd garnered pre-sale interest already and planned to release it as an e-book and online course in a few weeks time.

She opened her bullet journal and colored in a 'productivity square' for 'Instagram presence,' then another for 'eat a healthy dinner,' which was mostly true, then turned to a newly decorated page, blank but for the elaborate title 'Flipside, Week 1.' She had sections for 'projects completed,' 'to do list,' 'brand awareness,' and 'notes.' She also sold an online course on focused productivity through bullet journaling.

That night, as she smoothed retinol cream into her face and listened to David Facetiming with someone about the 'match,' Amanda looked in the mirror and whispered her affirmations: "You are strong, you are smart, you can do this."

The next morning, David had already gotten up to go to the gym, Amanda remembered a vague kiss on her forehead. She had one more day until filming began in earnest and she did not intend to waste it.

Her mom texted: *Still want to meet at Patty's?*

Of course! Amanda replied.

The mother daughter duo had been going to Patty's Hair Nails N' More for years. The salon's aesthetic embraced the 80s in a kitsch meets glam sort of way. They still did neon acrylics and big hair, large glass block partitions separated the spaces, accented with deep pink and purple lighting, everything had a daytime at the club feel. When you walked in, you were greeted by a velvet painting of Dolly Parton framed on the wall and outlined in twinkle lights. The receptionist at the front desk checked you in and offered you a mimosa. Everything was leopard print and Patty herself reigned supreme with her tight mini dresses and fake tits. They even kept an old school tanning bed in the back. Amanda loved it, it felt like going to your cool aunt's house and letting her give you a makeover.

Amanda arrived at Patty's at the same time as her mom, they embraced and went inside. Complimentary mimosas in hand and feet in the pedicure spa, they finally had space to chat under the dayglo lights.

"Sooo," her mother drawled, "How's it going with the house?"

"It's going. You know Daddy helped me find a plumber. Plus, he said he'd come by to help with some of the demo work. It's really not bad, a little bit of floorboard replacement, some water damage, a raccoon was living in the attic, but I already dealt with that. Mostly, it will be interior design, that's what the show wants to see anyway."

"You *do* have an eye for color."

"Plus, it's going to be a great launchpad for my brand."

Her mother visibly cringed, then tried to cover up her reaction by taking a sip of the mimosa.

"What?"

"Well, honey. Are you still planning on keeping up with this life coach stuff? Part of the reason Daddy wanted to help buy this house for you was so you and David could get a good start."

Amanda blushed, she didn't like admitting she'd asked her parents for the money to buy the house. She hadn't even told David, he wouldn't have approved, but their finances were still separate and she took her parents out to a nice dinner without him. She just wanted it so badly, to have something of her own, and her parents had seemed so effusive when she'd asked. "We'd love to help you," they'd cried, giving her early access to a portion of the trust they'd set up for her. Only now it felt like a barrier between them, something she hadn't anticipated since the money was always intended for her.

"David has his own business interests and I have mine. Consider it an investment in *my* future."

"I just thought it might finally be time."

"For what?"

"For you and David to finally start a family, tie the knot, get on with it."

"We're happy how we are."

"Look, I love you, but no one is gonna buy the cow if they can get the milk for free."

"Am I the cow?"

Her mother shrugged delicately and Amanda realized her mimosa was empty, someone brought her another and she scowled into the pool of scented water where flower petals swirled around her calves like the remnants of a bride's grand entrance.

Amanda opted for a gel manicure rather than acrylics as she anticipated getting her hands at least moderately dirty in the days to come, not too dirty she hoped. She chose a dusky mauve.

"Let's splurge on eyelash extensions, I'll buy," her mom offered.

Patty's ladies were more than happy to accommodate and, two hours and several mimosas later, both mom and daughter emerged from the salon pleasantly tipsy.

"You're going to be great, you'll win, just don't get too stressed, it's not good for your skin."

Amanda went home feeling burdened by something she couldn't quite put a finger on. David looked up from his video game when she walked in.

"Wow! You look like one of those Big Eyes paintings."

"Is it bad?"

"No, they're just very va-va-voom. Aw, fuck you!"

"What?"

"I'm playing the new *Call of Duty*, sorry, you look good."

Amanda walked into the kitchen and put three chlorophyll drops in a glass of water to combat the mimosas. She swallowed the grassy potion in one gulp. That night she tried to sleep on her back so as not to crush the eyelashes that felt heavy on her face.

She arrived at the house early, hair carefully curled and pushed back with an artful headband. She wanted to make sure to arrive before anyone else was scheduled to be there. The successful entrepreneur always starts their day early, a line from her productivity journal, and her morning routine was essential to her productivity.

However, despite her best efforts, she noticed an unmarked white van out front. The plumber, she thought jubilantly. She swung the door open anticipating a positive start to the day and debuting her successes, along with her new eyelashes, in her end of day one video log. Instead, she came face to face with a ladder and two men she did not recognize surveying the entirety of her living room.

"Um, excuse me. Who are you?"

"We're with production," the first man answered. The second man on the ladder looked visibly irritated and began climbing down.

"What are you doing?"

"Double checking the interior for shooting angles."

"And?"

"Everything looks in order. The rest of the team will be along in a few hours."

The pair of men quickly packed up and left without further explanation.

The entire encounter left her feeling frazzled and uncomfortable, not the best first day vibe. The pants she'd chosen to wear were too tight and she wanted to pick her wedgie, but felt as though she was no longer alone in the space. She retreated instead to the bathroom that still stank faintly of sewage and breathed deeply through her mouth.

Amanda looked in the mirror and repeated her affirmations: "You are strong, you are smart, you can do this." Then, she picked her wedgie.

She returned to the kitchen, opened the bottled oat milk latte she'd brought from home, and set up her laptop on the chipped and faded avocado formica countertop. She dumped her supplies next to it and referenced her bullet journal — the plumber was scheduled for 8:00 AM and production was supposed to come by at 10:00 AM to do a day one check in. She made a notation of her mood by drawing a sad face in the AM box for Monday. She shut her notebook again and put her ambient chillwave playlist on Spotify to calm her nerves. She felt a potent craving for one of the clove cigarettes she smoked in college.

The plumber arrived at 8:15 and Amanda was grateful for something to do. She showed him around the two bathrooms, answered questions about the age of the house and its general upkeep.

"This won't take much," the plumber answered, he wore a black tool belt that sagged down his thin hips, "Just a little blockage. I can run a snake down both pipes, have it flushing as good as new by lunchtime. It looks like the pipes are still pretty new."

"The construction company said they replaced the 'guts' of the house: water heater, air conditioning, pipes, and roof tiles when it was still a part of the new development concept, pre-bankruptcy, of course."

The plumber nodded, staring into the abyss of her eventual guest toilet.

"Yup, I'd say they did a fairly good job. Nothing fancy, but it's all there. Lemme go get my kit."

He returned with a medieval looking device, a long metal corkscrew on the end of a longer metal cord attached to a crank. He set about shoving the thing into the bowels of her house and Amanda logged into her laptop, trying to ignore the gurgling and splashing sounds, the squeaking of wet rubber soles on the linoleum floor.

She was planning to do the floors and counters herself, she'd ordered a ton of bamboo flooring from a lumber liquidation website. It wasn't quite the color she'd envisioned, but at ten cents a square foot, it could be bright orange for all she cared. She figured the quickest thing to do would be to begin tearing out the carpet in the master bedroom, plus it would be a great first impression when production did arrive.

Using a claw hammer, Amanda began to unhook the ancient, raggedy carpet from the staples in the wall. She appreciated that it used to be an attractive shag, but times had to change, and she ripped it up without remorse. It was therapeutic, if a little sweaty. Oh well, Amanda thought, it's reality TV after all.

The plumber excused his way into the master bathroom and repeated his splashing and gurgling process on the other toilet. He left footprints along the freshly exposed concrete floor.

With much effort, Amanda carried the carpet in large swatches out to a miniature dumpster she'd rented in preparation for the light demo. Just as she'd dumped the last square into the metal container, she saw another unmarked white van pull up beside the plumber's truck. He was re-loading the snake and she watched him chat up the camera man, they exchanged business cards. Word of mouth branding, so old school, Amanda thought.

The camera men came in and started setting up. Everything happened quickly and soon the entire house was awash in lights.

"Just ignore us, just act natural," they repeated.

Amanda smoothed her hair and tried not to look at the camera as she walked back and forth to the dumpster in the yard.

"We're not even here," they kept telling her.

Finally, someone from production pulled her aside and put a mic on her. They sat her in the kitchen and queried her on the first day, the emotions, the highs and lows.

"Well, you know, it's definitely a rush to finally get started."

"Don't say 'finally,'" the production assistant suggested.

"Why?"

"It makes it sound like the show kept you waiting."

"Well, it did."

"Right…"

"Right."

"Let's try again."

And so it went for about an hour. When they finally decided they had enough 'first day' footage, the van loaded up as quickly as they arrived. The production assistant reminded her, "Since we're still doing the thirty day challenge thing, we'll be back next Monday for a sneak peak of what you've done so far. We like to have several in-progress shots leading up to the final reveal."

At the end of the first day, she'd pulled up most of the

carpet and the plumbing situation had been rectified. Amanda felt the momentary thrill of marking both things off in her bullet journal. Still, there had been the minor disappointment that she'd had to interview alone. Her father hadn't shown up and David had just sent a thumbs up emoji text. She knew he was busy at work, but it stung all the same. Aside from the plumber, she'd been alone.

She sat down in the kitchen and put her head in her hands and rubbed her eyes, something she tried not to do for fear of wrinkles, but it felt cathartic, to press her knuckles into her eyes until she saw stars. She remembered the eyelash extensions a little too late, blinking open her red and watery eyes to click through some of the story posts on Instagram.

Amanda checked the #Flipside hashtag to see what the other participants were sharing. The family posted a lot, their kids were sitting on the floor in diapers and pull ups painting the bottom of their living room walls a robin's egg blue. She scrolled past and saw another couple replicating a shinier version of *American Gothic*. She flipped her phone face down onto the table and stared at the ceiling.

A tickle in the air caught her attention and Amanda whipped around, half-expecting someone from production to have come back in, but there was no one. Goosebumps raised on her arms and her bladder suddenly felt too full.

Tomorrow, I will put blinds on the windows, she decided, and added it to her bullet journal.

Over the next week, Amanda spent more and more time at the house. She didn't answer the phone unless it was someone from Flipside production or one of the many people she was pleading for help.

Her father did eventually come over with two men who had recently remodeled her parents' kitchen and helped with the initial direction for the installation of her bamboo flooring. He didn't stay much longer than to drop off an everything bagel with cream cheese and kiss her on the cheek.

"Proud of you, Duckie," he called, before rushing off to somewhere else. Amanda's father existed in her life as a constant blur of motion, but his sudden appearance buoyed her into action for the remainder of the week.

The two men worked steadily through the stacks of bamboo that had been delivered to Amanda's front porch. Unable to move it herself, she'd panicked, worried about the HOA, and then begged her father for help. She made sure to make note of his gallant assistance in her end of day video log.

Somewhat bored, Amanda sat watching the men cut each bamboo piece with precision and then apply them to the concrete with wood glue. She kept offering to help, but they waved her away laughing, so she made them iced tea and watched YouTube videos on how to install a concrete countertop. The avocado formica was her next adversary.

Her primary motivation for choosing concrete finishes over marble or granite was money. Amanda spent almost a full day online, she studied how to create the mould, pour the concrete, and smooth it over. It looked easy enough and, the following morning, she bought all the requisite supplies at Home Depot.

The floor guys watched as she hammered together a mould and sealed it with silicone so it wouldn't leak. They leant her a level and helped her lift the container of mixed concrete over the lip. Amanda watched with satisfaction as it filled the mould like a lava flow. She smoothed the top with a trowel and backed away slowly to let it all dry.

Finally, after the chic wooden blinds had done little to

make her feel less observed, Amanda called her college friend, Sienna, to come over and sage the place.

"I just feel like there's some negative energy that needs to be cleansed. I don't want to completely negate the history here, but sometimes when I'm alone in a room I get the heebie jeebies."

"You want ghosts, but friendly ghosts."

"Exactly!"

Sienna came over on a day production showed up unannounced. The assistant was delighted to film Sienna walking barefoot through the house wearing a caftan and gold headband, holding aloft a bundle of sage and asking everyone to manifest positive vibes.

"You need to stay here and imbue the house with good energy," Sienna told her later as they split a bottle of kombucha at the, fully dried and rustic chic, concrete countertop.

"I feel like my own energy is so frazzled lately, I'm not sure it will work."

"Just watch a movie on your laptop, make some popcorn, and really try to envision it as a home. You have a vision don't you?"

Amanda allowed herself to drift for a moment, to imagine the newly sanded and re-finished French doors opening onto a back patio with the hot tub she so longed for, plants and twinkle lights inviting the outdoors back inside and creating a lush paradise. She'd visit her favorite plant nursery and choose hard to care for ferns and orchids, spend her mornings tending them and doing pilates in the extra bedroom. That would be the perfect office, she could use an entire wall as her vision board and work area and still have space for a yoga mat, an exercise bike, and her weights. Maybe she'd get a canopy bed in some pastel color everyone would hate, but she'd put up jacquard wallpaper and change their minds. She imagined two white bedside tables, she'd adorn one of them with a 1920's fringe lamp she always saw in thrift stores but never bought, the other side she'd pile high with romance novels and hide a stash of chocolate bars in the drawers, the non-vegan kind.

"I can already see you thinking about it. Just enter the home with those vibes in place and project them outward like pure white energy into the space."

Amanda nodded, it felt like sound advice. Sienna was the best energy healer in the Dallas Fort Worth metro area, after all. They finished the kombucha and talked of other things, eventually she thanked Sienna and went home to her downtown condo.

The days had started to run together and David had become another object in motion, a blur, always to and from work and the gym and meeting the boys for a drink. She entered the threshold of their modern abode with full intention of suggesting a movie night.

"Honey, I'm home," she announced in her full Ricky Ricardo impersonation.

No answer. Maybe he's out, she thought.

She went into the kitchen to get a vegan string cheese to hold her over until David resurfaced. It was then she first noticed the jars, stacks upon stacks of Mason jars layered in the fridge like a rainbow of questionable substances. How they'd escaped her before Amanda wasn't sure. Had she really been that busy?

She recognized the beets, now portioned out and assigned their own glass prisons, then perhaps green beans, some sort of fermenting pepper, and something that had turned a putrid shade of orange yellow she suspected could be peach, nectarine, radish?

The lights from the fridge backlit the science experiment that was now taking place in her kitchen as though it were a museum display. The variety of colors reminded her of her grandmother's depression glass collection.

There was no space for any other food and Amanda began to search, ultimately finding another dorm-sized refrigerator sitting on top of their washing machine. The bottom shelf was wholly taken over by a large bowl covered with foil, the pungency struck her immediately and she recalled his first attempts with kimchi, this had to be another cabbage experiment.

The rest of their food was crammed haphazardly onto the top shelf. She extracted a faux cheese stick from the mess and set it down on the counter. She went to the bathroom to wash her hands, only to discover a new scene of horrors. The bathtub was filled with sealed plastic tubs in various stages of bloat. Amanda vaguely remembered David mentioning he needed to 'burp the sauerkraut,' a concept she now more fully appreciated.

She gave her hands a cursory rinse before retreating to the living room. After her conversation with Sienna, their expensive modular couch felt angular and cold. Amanda supposed it was, they'd chosen such neutral modern furniture when they'd moved in together. Everything was gray or stone or slate or sand, named after nature without a trace of the outdoors' warmth. What was I thinking, she wondered, looking at her glass table with faux wood base. The base was meant to look as though her lumberjack husband had just cut down a tree and brought it to her as a gift, smoothed and polished, ready for display. Only she knew David had bought it at West Elm and the thought made her depressed.

By the time David got back from the gym, Amanda had

sunk as far into the sofa as the frame would allow and was deep into a *Real Housewives* rewatch.

"Hey, I didn't know you'd be back so early."

"Yeah, I wanted to see you."

He kissed her head and she pulled him in for a longer embrace, he recoiled.

"Don't, I'm all sweaty."

"That's okay."

He swatted at her hand and she pulled the gray, faux fur throw over her knees.

"Where are you going to shower anyway? The bathtub is full."

"Oh no, the sauerkraut!"

He disappeared and she turned the TV up. She wanted a glass of white wine very badly, but all David kept in the house was some 90 calorie gluten free beer and she just couldn't bring herself to pretend it was good. Instead, she watched rich women fight on their too large television mounted to a blank wall.

David reemerged smelling even worse than before.

"I thought you were going to shower?"

"Oh, yeah. The bathtub's full, I forgot."

He sat down on the couch, untroubled.

"Do we have to watch this?"

"It's almost over. Do you want to get something for dinner?"

"I thought we could order from that salad place we tried last week."

She sighed.

"What?"

"I don't want salad."

"Well, what do you want then Ms. Picky?"

"A steak."

"What?"

"I want a steak and some red wine and a side of French fries."

David laughed, "Come on. You know I can't have that."

"You didn't ask what you could have, you asked what I wanted."

"We aren't getting steak."

"Fine. Then order tofu fried rice. I don't want salad."

"What is wrong with you?"

"My entire apartment has turned into Fermentation Station and it stinks and you stink. Everything stinks! But I can't even open my own windows."

"Geez, I didn't know it bothered you so much."

"It's the entire fridge, and another fridge I didn't even know you bought, and a bathtub."

"It's my hobby," he pouted. "I don't complain about yours."

"Mine doesn't take over everything!"

"It doesn't?"

He got up and went into the bathroom where she assumed he had resorted to using the sink to wash. She sighed again, to herself this time, and used her phone to punch in an online delivery order for tofu fried rice, sautéed bok choy, and broccoli in black bean sauce. Once it arrived, they ate in silence, but he didn't ask her to change the television channel again.

Amanda packed an extra set of clothes and threw her pillow in the backseat of her car when she left in the blue pre-dawn of the next morning. She told herself this minor pre-planning was to follow Sienna's advice and spend a night in the house, to envision it more positively, more wholly.

As she approached the front door of the house, she immediately sensed something was wrong. The door wasn't locked and had been left slightly ajar, she picked up a rock from the flower bed and approached with it held aloft overhead.

"Hello?" Her own voice echoed back to her.

The house was mostly open plan now, so she only needed to throw open a couple of doors to determine there was no one's head present for her to smash. She felt a little disappointed and walked back into the living room. It was then she noticed the wall.

It looked as though someone had taken a hammer to the middle of it, haphazardly creating a series of potholes along the way from the front door to the dining area and out into the garden.

"What the fuck?" Amanda yelled.

The hammer had been discarded by the back door and she picked it up, it was the one her father had given her.

"Turned against me," she grumbled at the tool.

She looked everywhere, but couldn't find any other evidence of vandalism. Clearly, it was an act of minor vandalism. Kids, she assumed, bored teenagers. She considered calling the police, but it seemed an overreaction once she inspected the wall and saw that the holes were about six inches, not too large, and hadn't damaged any other structural features. She could fix it with a drywall patch, mud, and a fresh coat of paint, though it would take a while.

Luckily, Home Depot opens early, she thought. She bought the requisite supplies and an extra top bolt for the front door.

She made sure to also take a significant amount of video with her hand camera showing the damage and her repair process, she recorded a total of two hours worth of footage including her video journal at the end of the day. She didn't share anything on social media just in case the vandals knew her house was part of the show and might follow her online.

The whole ordeal left her feeling protective. This was *her* house, and she didn't appreciate that someone had violated it. Still she'd made her mind up about staying the night and had set up her laptop on a small stool in front of the plush green sofa she'd already purchased for the living room.

"It'll be like a sleepover, just me and you," she told the house.

She texted David: *Staying at the house tonight. Have some projects to finish up.*

He responded: *Okay.*

She didn't tell him about the drywall holes.

Later, Amanda realized she hadn't eaten much since her coffee and green juice hours ago at the condo. The supermarket was just down the street, though she'd never been there before.

The supermarket's parking lot was bustling with families and carts full of food and children. Amanda navigated her way into the fray and under the glaring intensity of the fluorescent lit compound. A Top 40 soundtrack from a decade prior played loudly over the din of carts and crying children. She and David usually shopped at the natural grocery store downtown or ordered their pre-packed meals online. Amanda couldn't remember the last time she'd been in a big box style store. She wandered down the aisles, reacquainting herself with brand name cereals and non-plant-based milks.

At last, she found herself leaning over the meat counter. Dallas was a place that valued steak and Amanda appreciatively appraised the butcher's offerings.

"Can I help you?" A man in a stained white coat and hair net asked her.

"No. Uh, yes, actually."

He didn't react, just waited for her to make the call.

"I'd like a filet mignon."

"Just one?"

"Yes, just one."

He weighed and wrapped it for her.

"Thank you."

She bought steak seasoning, potatoes, butter, coffee, half and half, eggs, hummus, pita chips, three bottles of kombucha, string cheese, a box of microwave popcorn, and a cheap bottle of red wine. The experience of choosing food for only herself was confusing. Initially she was overwhelmed by the deceptive feeling of not knowing her own tastes, but her preferences returned slowly and she felt a thrill as she grabbed an Almond Joy at the checkout register.

Night had fallen and the parking lot felt festive with its tall streetlamp and the flickering red taillights of fleeing shoppers. The truck next to Amanda's own car had several bumper stickers: *Keep Your California Outta My Texas* and *Keep Dallas Armed* were prominently featured. Perhaps not as festive as she'd thought.

The recently installed porch lights came on with the onset of dusk and Amanda smiled as she pulled into the circular driveway. The driveway itself made the whole front of the house feel more snug than a house at the end of a long straight drive. She felt safe and enclosed, though the newly installed bolt lock helped with that as well.

Amanda lingered for a long time in the kitchen preparing her simple steak and potatoes dinner. She sprinkled seasonings, melted butter, and listened to the seductive sizzling of pan frying, then poured herself a glass of wine. Drinking was another activity she rarely engaged in, she couldn't discern a Cabernet Sauvignon from a Merlot, but tonight it simply felt decadent to walk through a house she owned, in her pajamas, clasping a glass of wine to her breast as she played Lana del Rey. The wine tasted like cherries and chocolate, the house smelled savory and peppery, the bubbles of anxiety melted in her chest with the first bite of steak.

After dinner, she washed her few dishes, and carried the wine and Almond Joy to her nest on the couch. She was queuing up a true crime docuseries, then thought better of it, and put on a *Sex and the City* rerun instead. As she was pouring another glug of wine, a chill crept up her spine and her shoulders shuddered unbidden.

Amanda whipped around, but no one was there. Just her and Carrie and her silent indulgences. It's probably just my body readjusting to meat, she told herself lightly, nothing to worry about. But the softest robotic sound answered in response, like the buzzing of a beetle or a light fuse. Again, she told herself it was the guilt, the steak, the alcohol, just relax.

Still, the saying 'someone walking over your grave,' slid into her mind. When anyone got random chills as a child, her grandmother would always respond with her rote saying to remind them all of their impending death. As a child, she always pictured a cartoonish gravestone with her own name written across it. The picture Amanda conjured now was one of David walking back and forth across the expensive flooring in their condo.

"You have enough, you are enough," she repeated to herself and tapped her collarbone to calm her vagus nerve. Then, she turned on her show, finished the Almond Joy, and fell asleep feeling as though everything was alright with the world despite the fact that she hadn't used her bullet journal in three days.

Sometime around 3:00 AM, Amanda's phone buzzed several times in quick succession. She awoke with a fluttery panicked feeling in her chest and flung her arm out to swat at whatever bug had invaded her rest. The motion sent her rolling off the side of the sofa that she had misjudged to be as wide as her king sized condo bed. From her newfound perspective on the floor, Amanda realized there were no shadow bugs and picked up her phone.

There were several notifications, some popping up even now, and she began to scroll through her messages app. First, a single number texted her an ominous warning, "you're being watched" with a link.

Surely it was spam, she thought, intending to block everyone, disregard the entire thing, and go back to bed. That is, until someone in the group chat referenced Flipside.

She clicked on the link from the first text message. It took her to a livestream feed of mostly darkness, at the bottom she could see it had been recording for some time. A small blue dot was moving. She tried to zoom in with her fingers to discern any other information and saw a woman, vaguely illuminated in the halo of blue, peering down at her screen. She was sitting on the floor, back against the sofa, a sofa that looked quite similar to her own. It had to be one of those weird Twitch sleeping streams or something. Amanda tried again in vain to zoom in further, but was thwarted, she threw her head back in frustration and the woman in the video did the same.

Wait.

She raised her right arm and saw the action mirrored in

the pale light. Amanda stood and ran to the kitchen, she turned on the lights in the freshly opened up living room and dining area and saw her bamboo floors and concrete countertop clearly on the phone screen.

Her stomach clenched. This has to be a sick joke, she decided.

Her shaking hand opened the group chat and one of the anonymous numbers had typed: *I checked the Flipside contract, we did agree to 24/7 surveillance.*

What is going on? She typed. *I just got a weird text with a livestream of me? Is this a joke.*

Several people were typing back.

No joke.

They've been watching us the whole time.

We all signed off on it.

Amanda realized now she was talking to the other Flipside contestants, that one of them had texted her.

Who found out? She asked.

Carly in Indiana.

Yeah, they accidentally BCCed me in an email because I guess their lawyers name is also Carly. It had links to everyones livestreams. I sent them out.

Amanda felt sick, though she might reasonably be able to attribute that to the beef. The messages began arriving quickly now, one after the other.

It makes you think what else they may have done for the show.

What do you mean?

Well, last week someone stole our mailbox. It was custom made, something we'd spent a lot of time working on. It definitely would have been on camera.

That's so weird, someone uprooted our freshly planted flower bed!

Someone put holes in the sheetrock, I thought it was just vandals, Amanda added.

It seemed as though most of the contestants had received some sort of minor setback.

It feels like a lot of coincidences, too many.

As more texts and speculation rolled in, Amanda followed the visual on her livestream to discern where the camera was. She dragged a kitchen chair over and inspected the corner of the living room closest to the door. They really did have an expansive view, especially since she'd made everything open. There it was, the sound, a little robotic buzz as the lens adjusted to focus on her in close up. The camera itself was tiny, she'd never have seen it. It was the same color as the ceiling.

"Found you," she told the off-white spot.

The rest of the early morning consisted of texting out their impotent rage at being watched. Amanda realized that some people may have done far worse things in front of the camera than her, her worst crime was certainly her recent binge fest. As the texts rolled in, it seemed some of the others had disciplined their children, had sex on the newly acquired furniture, violently argued, used cheaper materials than what they'd claimed, and a bevy of other things that would probably make production pleased to intersperse between the more sanitized cuts of their video journals. The show runners were preventing the contestants from curating the experience.

I'll have to take the vegetarian bit off my Instagram profile, was Amanda's last thought before putting her phone on its do not disturb setting and going back to sleep.

The next morning, she went back to the condo, she

needed to talk to David, see what he thought. She caught him just as he was getting ready to leave for the gym.

"Hey," she began.

"Hi. I'm already late, so…"

"I just wanted to talk really quick."

He set down his gym back as an indication for her to go on.

"So, something really creepy happened last night."

"Yeah? Did Sienna's sage not get all the ghosts?"

"No, this was actually creepy. I got this anonymous text and it was a link to a livestream, but the livestream was of me."

"What?"

"Right?! So, then I see the person who sent it to me also added me to a group chat and I realized it was the other contestants from *Flipside*! Apparently they had livestreams on all of us and we signed off on it in the contract, or that's what they said anyway, I didn't check," she was rushing now, "I found the camera in the ceiling. And everyone else had all these little things go wrong or get stolen, like the sheetrock that was damaged with the hammer at my house."

"When did that happen?"

"The other day. So, what do you think I should do?"

"About the sheetrock?"

"No! About this whole discovery!"

David was leaning against the door now, away from her, and crossed his arms over his chest.

"What can you do if you signed off on it?"

"It feels violating."

"It is. But you knew they'd try to dig stuff up. I told you, it's all scripted and planned. And when things are going too well they come in and literally take a hammer to it because that's better TV."

Amanda could tell from his tone that he felt vindicated by the whole thing rather than concerned and it annoyed her.

"Several of the people did really inappropriate stuff and didn't realize they'd been caught on camera."

"Well, I won't worry about that with you," he laughed.

"I'm glad this is all so funny to you."

"I'm sorry Amanda, it's a little silly. From the minute you signed up for it, I just felt like you were deluding yourself into another little scheme, another way to get yourself noticed without actually doing much work."

"What does that mean?"

"It means that you like the appearance of busyness rather than actually being busy."

"I started my own brand and I've been doing a lot of the labor on this house! Design work starts next week and I have all the furniture picked out and ready to stage."

"Appearance," David held up his finger.

"As though you don't think appearances matter. Enjoy your trip to the gym," she hissed. "I'm going to shower and then back to my delusion."

She walked off, he didn't follow, and, as soon as the hot water hit her face, she began to cry.

During the last week of the competition, Amanda was more or less living in the house. She worked around the clock, to get things repaired, painted, shining. Her dad dropped by with another bagel on his way to work, they discussed drywall, her mother called and told her they were proud of her. Amanda texted often with Carly, another contestant she'd connected with in the group chat, who was remodeling a farmhouse in rural Indiana but was also a retired Army photographer with two German Shepherds. Eventually, the initial ire of the group chat lessened and turned into acceptance after a heated Zoom call with production in which they were promised 'favorable edits' to the secretive footage. Amanda still dutifully logged her video journals each day even though she knew some other teams had stopped.

"So, it's day twenty-six and all I have left to do is finish re-tiling one corner of the master bathroom. Everything else is done, I can't believe it! My parents are coming to help me stage the house this weekend and then we'll be all ready for the reveal."

She turned off the camera and her fifty watt smile and sank back into the kitchen chair. She lied, she'd finished the tile earlier, but wanted to seem as though she was working until the last minute. The dining room was dim, but she could admire the open kitchen in the blue light. The cabinets now had glass doors and new hardware and everything was whitewashed. The cement countertop looked more expensive than she'd thought it would and all the linoleum was now bamboo flooring. It looked just as she'd imagined, ready for someone to move in and fill the cabinets with their Le Cruset collection. The thought made her a little sad.

Did you see this? Carly texted with a link to an obituary.

Amanda clicked through and read:

Jessica Fairchild passed away at the age of 48, (haha — only the Devil will know her real age when they inevitably meet), in Los Angeles, California. A devout atheist and somewhat reformed party girl, Jessica spent her last few years caring for her dogs more than most people. She had a somewhat successful movie career and a very successful theater career because she could project her voice at decibels that might kill a mortal man, every director's dream. Anyway, this lovable harpy was my best friend and I will miss her desperately.

Thanks for the memories, for always having the best weed (although that was mostly because of the cancer), and rest in the most peaceful position you can find. — Ferdy Alstadt.

Ms. Fairchild requested to be cremated and there will be no public memorial held. Instead, she requested donations be made to Old Mutts Adoption Agency in Los Angeles.

Amanda's stomach dropped. In her heart of hearts, she'd hoped that Jessica might notice the house on *Flipside* and reach out to her with words of admiration, thanking her for giving the house a second (or third, or fourth) chance. Instead, she was face to face with an online obit, albeit a rather pithy one.

She texted Carly back: *I hadn't seen it. Gutted!*

Sorry girl. <3 Just stay positive, you're going to kill it!

She and Carly hadn't shared many photos of their own projects, it was still a competition after all, but they'd discussed possibly doing a meetup after the show ended.

Amanda read the obituary again. She wondered if anyone in her own life would ever see her as fully as Ferdy seemed to have seen Jessica. At the moment, it felt doubtful.

David had texted her asking if she was coming home, but Amanda didn't respond and instead spent the next hour or so scrolling through Jessica Fairchild's wikipedia, then reading people's personal farewells on Twitter. She considered posting her own, but thought it might be too attention grabby, considering she was still in production for the show.

She texted her mom: *Feeling lonely tonight.*

The response came quickly: *Well, you made your bed hun. You'll have to lie in it.*

Per usual, their conversation didn't make her feel any

better. She heated up a box of frozen chicken nuggets and fell asleep on the couch.

The next morning was her first staging day and Amanda rose early to hide any evidence of her sleeping there. She knew some of the other contestants were staying in their homes as well, but it felt like some kind of betrayal to tell anyone, especially considering how unsupportive her mom had been when they went out for Tex Mex the night before.

"You're throwing a perfectly good relationship down the drain!"

"I just feel like we are becoming two different people."

"Different people can make things work. I thought y'all were going to start a family."

"We never said that, *you* said that. Besides, he has a family, it's just jars of pickles instead of me."

The pickles and soccer, not to mention her own feelings, were things she simply needed to get over, apparently, the 'meat thing,' as her father referred to it, was something they'd have to work on.

"No grandchildren of mine are gonna eat rabbit food. They need meat to keep their iron levels up and build protein."

"There's no grandchildren at all, Dad."

"We'll figure out the meat thing."

She'd left with a doggie bag of chips and queso and a distinct heaviness, brought on most likely by the seemingly insurmountable stress and also the chimichanga she'd eaten.

The moving van delivered all of the furniture around ten. They put pieces in the rooms she'd marked down, everything still wrapped in plastic. She'd picked most of it out previously at the interior designer warehouse her previous job had used. The deal was that she could borrow it for a fee, then sell it to whoever ended up buying the house, otherwise it all went back.

Amanda spent the afternoon directing the placement of everything and a good part of the early evening unwrapping the furniture, reassembling the few things that needed attention, and dragging furniture around on washcloths so as not to scratch the floor. She'd chosen an emerald green velvet sofa and loveseat for the living room, a very avant garde coffee table made of plexiglass sat in between them, its bottom wove back and forth like an accordion, the top was flat, and all of it entirely clear. It was one of Amanda's favorite pieces in the collection she'd chosen. She had everything from the four poster bed she'd dreamed of to white plates with gold bands that matched all the other white dinnerware.

The house still needed a few things: linens, pillows, some plants, and art. But she had a gallerist coming the following day to install a couple of well placed art pieces. These also would go back to the gallery after being featured on the *Flipside* finale.

Her astrology calendar app informed Amanda that tonight was a full moon. The app also informed her it was a night for accepting gratitude and fulfillment and manifesting that which you would like to bring more abundantly into your life.

She decided impulsively to have a little full moon ritual, something Sienna had told her about. She had previously suggested that on the house's first full moon Amanda light a candle and write ten things she was grateful for and ten things she wanted to be grateful for in the future. Then, she was to burn the list.

Amanda turned off all the lights in the house, she lit a lavender candle from Whole Foods, and sat down to try and put words to her gratitude. The first list proved difficult and she realized she'd omitted anything about her relationships and chose to focus more on the intangible, the feelings of accomplishment and pride she had about the house project.

Her future gratitude list flowed more easily. She wanted a place that felt like home, fulfilling friendships, and more space for creativity. She also wrote in tiny print: I miss my office job. She hadn't expressed that feeling to anyone, but she had loved working at the real estate office and speaking with people every day. Life coaching was something David had introduced her to once she'd started pumping him up about vegetarianism, it was something her mother supported because it kept her mostly home with the imaginary brood they were going to have, but, deep down, Amanda wanted to work in an office again. She wanted to channel her empathic tendencies toward helping people achieve their dreams of finding a home, or maybe she wanted to help design the interiors.

And I am going to manifest it, she told herself as she lit the corner of the paper on fire with the lavender candle, then watched it burn in the bottom of her new undermounted farmhouse style sink.

She walked outside into the yard and looked up at the full, round moon. The yard itself was illuminated and long shadows were cast across it as though sentinels stood guard just outside the fence line. It was all very well-manicured but lacked the soul Amanda wanted to inject. She'd kept it a neutral palette for now. Then, in the distance and for the first time, she noticed sparkling lights.

Fireflies, she thought. In all her years living in Dallas, Amanda hadn't seen them but a handful of times. She watched them blink on and off against the shadowy silhouette of the hedges.

A memory bubbled up of kayaking with her parents in Tomales Bay. The bay itself was grey and cloudy, but her father insisted that they strain themselves against the wind. Amanda was small then and often stopped, letting her arms loll at her sides while her dad steered them both expertly through the waves. Her mom refused to get in the boat for fear of getting her hairdo wet and stayed at their cabin in front of the potbelly stove.

They bought a bag of fresh oysters and grilled them over the fire, Amanda remembered the shock of the texture, the briny taste. Later, her father woke her up with a gentle nudge once the sun had gone down and their campfire was mostly ash. "Come on, let's go," he put her in a lifejacket, and she blearily assisted him in pushing the kayak back out into the bay. Once they were centered and calm, the water and silence lapping around them, her dad encouraged her to put her hand in the water.

Someone at the boathouse told them there might be sharks in the bay at this time of year and her child's mind had conjured up all manner of horrors, but her father assured her it was safe. She trailed her fingers just along the surface and watched as a soft, sparkling light trailed behind them like spun gold. Amanda gasped. The bay was filled with phosphorescent algae, her dad explained, but she'd always privately maintained that it was magic.

She watched now as the fireflies blinked out and disappeared, one by one, until she was alone in the darkness.

That night, Amanda made the bed with the new linens and snuggled down into it like she was placing herself inside an envelope. She lay awake for hours imagining every different thing she could be.

The next morning was time for finishing touches. She set out fake plants from Target, crystal candle holders and coffee table books from Goodwill, and directed the hanging of the art gallery installations.

At the front, near the window, she set up a white ceramic sculpture of the heads of three women intertwined. Beneath them, there were only waves, above the waves, their heads connected in a circle as though they were telling secrets. Amanda had seen it at the gallery and loved it. On the bedroom walls and in the living room she had chosen two aquatic colored abstract pieces. The first one began in the bottom left corner with an angry dark blue, almost black, and faded out in sporadic strokes to almost white in the top right corner. She hung that one above the sofa. In the bedroom, she chose the soft blue painting, still with rough, almost angry, paintbrush strokes. Amanda found it calming, a piece she could come home to every day and agree with the general mood.

She recorded her final video journal and readied everything for production. She even gave a cheeky wave to the corner camera. She texted Carly: *I think it's done.* Carly texted back immediately: *Congrats!* The *Flipside* group chat was blowing up with last minute disasters, panic attacks, and reminders to take deep breaths. Some of the messages got catty and Amanda made popcorn topped with slices of Parmesan cheese and spent her evening flipping back and forth between her phone and *Bravo*.

Her texts to David had dwindled to simple: *yes, no, okay* over the past few evenings and she suspected he'd forgotten the show was about to conclude.

After the third day of monosyllables, she sent him a long

email, detailing how she felt they'd grown apart and had different goals. She finished by wishing him the best. Her fingers twitched for just a moment, a slight hesitation, before she pressed send. When she probed her feelings, they felt like an already healing bruise.

An hour later, he posted to social media: *Dumped via email, the long shadow of technology extends ever outward.* He only emailed her back to coordinate a time for her to pick up the rest of her things, assuring her he would be out of the condo.

On the final filming day, the production vans pulled up in all of their chaotic glory. Amanda barely had a moment to say hello before they were upon her, lights were installed in every room and at every conceivable angle, they ooh-ed and ahh-ed over the transformation, congratulated her, then sent her to have light hair and makeup.

Her mom texted: *Today's the day!*

Her dad: *Proud of you, Duckie.*

Amanda submitted to the ministrations of the crew as they curled her hair and applied a little blush.

"You need stage makeup, those lights will wash you right out."

Amanda closed her eyes and let them dust soft peaches and pinks over her eyelids, her cheeks, the tip of her nose. She sparkled and shone in the mirror of the vanity set up she'd picked out for the master bedroom weeks before.

"Alright, let's go!"

She walked back out into the open living room and the production assistant encouraged her, "Walk us through it. What were the highlights and the challenges, what was the biggest transformation, the biggest money makers?"

Amanda found it surprisingly easy to take them on a tour of the house. She spoke with confidence of her triumphs, mostly the decor, and some of the challenges, like pouring a concrete counter for the first time and *someone* busting a hole in the sheetrock. Production had the composure to look shocked at that anecdote.

"Do you feel a sense of relief now that it's complete?"

"I feel like a house is a project that's never quite done and, if you approach it in that manner, it's both fun and rewarding. So, there's relief, but also a feeling like 'oh if I could just tweak *one more thing.*'"

The assistant smiled, then nodded to the cameraman. They stopped rolling and shook hands.

"We do want to get a few establishing shots of the front of the house, curb appeal and all that, and it has that great circular drive. Do you mind?"

"Not at all." As she walked out, she noticed one of the other assistants carrying a ladder and switching from one foot to the other impatiently. She leaned over to him, "Make sure you don't damage the paint job when you take down that spy cam."

His eyes widened and his mouth gaped like a fish, as he searched for the appropriate response, but Amanda just flipped her hair and walked out front where she posed in the circular driveway for the *Flipside's* millions of viewers, smiling with her hand on her hip like a retro Texas Barbie. Production ended up using the image as a promo shot when they advertised the show.

When the show aired a couple of months later, Amanda watched most of the episodes from the house's living room, texting her *Flipside* group chat, and then Carly separately to gossip about the group chat. She and David split up quietly and mostly amicably, neither of them had fought for the relationship. He'd gotten a roommate who liked Madrid's soccer team, they argued about it a lot, and with more passion than David had ever shown her. Still, somehow, alone, she now felt less alone.

On the final day of staging, she'd taken the card of one of the women who had helped her set up furniture. Amanda emailed her and eventually applied to work at the same interior design studio that had staged her house and spent the intervening weeks shutting down her life coaching business and transitioning into a new career.

"You have such an eye for color," they told her.

Magazines called to interview her and requested to photograph the house. Amanda said yes to all of them, she even had a feature in *Texas Monthly*. People she hadn't spoken to since high school found her on Facebook to congratulate her, a few tried to take her out on a date. She said no to all of them.

She invited her parents over for the finale and they all sat on her velvet couch and held hands as the show did a recap montage of everyone's journey. No one knew yet who the *Flipside* winner would be. In previous seasons, the host would show up at your house with a van full of production and lights, like *Publisher's Clearing House*, and film you crying. Amanda did not relish this aspect of it, but she did want to win. She wanted the money, the prestige, the 'atta girl of having accomplished something. She'd done a deep cleaning the day before in preparation and now sat in between her mom and dad watching as production illuminated a house that was decidedly not hers.

The family with two young children came out dressed impeccably, their hands shielding their faces against the onslaught of production lights. The children screamed and clapped while the parents clasped one another and cried. Amanda's unkind thought was that they made for more wholesome television. Her mom began to rub her back and her father stood abruptly. Amanda knew he wanted to feel purposeful, that he needed something to do with his hands.

He asked, "Okay, who needs a beer?" And returned with three bottles of Shiner Bock.

"It's okay. You did a great job. It's really beautiful!"

"I know, Mom. Thanks."

"You can probably sell it for a pretty profit."

"I don't think I am going to."

"You'll for sure make money off of it," her dad insisted.

"No, I mean… I think I want to keep it."

Both of her parents looked unsurprised.

"I know I put all my life coaching money and some of yours into it, but I really think I want to live here. I have a steady paycheck now, so I can still pay back the trust if you want."

"We thought you might want to keep it," her mom replied.

Her father raised his beer bottle, "Onward and upward, Duck!"

The screen on the television continued to play interviews and montages of the entire *Flipside* season. As her parents chatted about the other contestants, Amanda returned to her imagined backyard. She could see her family together grilling burgers and cutting a watermelon into slices, maybe there would even be children, eventually. She imagined them pulling at her pant legs, spitting watermelon seeds, and running through the yard with sparklers trailing stars behind them. *I can manifest it*, she thought.

About the Author

Abigail Stewart is a fiction writer from Berkeley, California. She is the author of two previous books, *The Drowned Woman* and *Assemblage*.

About the Publisher

Whisk(e)y Tit is committed to restoring degradation and degeneracy to the literary arts. We work with authors who are unwilling to sacrifice intellectual rigor, unrelenting playfulness, and visual beauty in our literary pursuits, often leading to texts that would otherwise be abandoned in today's largely homogenized literary landscape. In a world governed by idiocy, our commitment to these principles is an act of civil service and civil disobedience alike.